SHADOW

SATAN'S FURY: MEMPHIS CHAPTER

L. WILDER

Shadow
Satan's Fury MC Memphis

This book is a work of fiction. Some of the places named in the book are actual places found in Paris, TN. The names, characters, brands, and incidents are either the product of the author's imagination or are used fictitiously. The author acknowledges the trademarked status and owners of various products and locations referenced in this work of fiction, which have been used without permission. The publication or use of these trademarks is not authorized, associated with, or sponsored by the trademark owners.

 Warning: This book is intended for readers 18 years or older due to bad language, violence, and explicit sex scenes.

L. Wilder www.lwilderbooks.net

Cover Model: Travis

Photographer- Wander Photography

Cover Design: Mayhem Cover Creations
www.facebook.com/MayhemCoverCreations

Editor: Lisa Cullinan

Proofreader- Rose Holub www.facebook.com/ReadbyRose/

Teasers & Banners: Gel Ytayz at Tempting Illustrations

Personal Assistant: Natalie Weston PA

NEWSLETTER SIGNUP: http://eepurl.com/dvSpW5 Sign up for latest updates on L. Wilder Books and for a chance to win signed copies and more.

Catch up with the entire Satan's Fury MC Series today! All books are FREE with Kindle Unlimited!

Summer Storm (Satan's Fury MC Novella)

Maverick (Satan's Fury MC #1)

Stitch (Satan's Fury MC #2)

Cotton (Satan's Fury MC #3)

Clutch (Satan's Fury MC #4)

Smokey (Satan's Fury MC #5)

Big (Satan's Fury #6)

Two Bit (Satan's Fury #7)

Diesel (Satan's Fury #8)

Blaze (Satan's Fury Memphis Chapter)

Shadow (Satan's Fury Memphis Chapter)

Damaged Goods- (The Redemption Series Book 1- Nitro)

Max's Redemption (The Redemption Series Book 2- Max)

Inferno (Devil Chasers #1)

Smolder (Devil Chaser #2)

Ignite (Devil Chasers #3)

Consumed (Devil Chasers #4)

Combust (Devil Chasers #5)

My Temptation (The Happy Endings Collection #1)

Bring the Heat (The Happy Endings Collection #2)

His Promise (The Happy Endings Collection #3)

PROLOGUE

It was always the same.

Night after night.

As soon as I got in bed and closed my eyes, my mind would start drifting back to my childhood. It wasn't something that I liked to think about, but I just couldn't seem to help myself. With each moment that passed, I could feel myself being pulled into an old familiar nightmare—one that I'd had many times before. A cold sweat washed over me as all those old childhood feelings of fear and helplessness came rushing back, causing my pulse to race and my breath to quicken. I'd tried to fight it. I'd tried to force my mind in a new direction, but I couldn't stop those dreadful memories from flooding back, haunting me as they forced me to remember a time I was desperate to forget. I'd tossed back and forth, trying to shake myself free from the nightmare's hold, but it was no use. No matter what I did, I'd find myself back in that house, listening to those gut-wrenching cries of anguish and feeling completely helpless to make it stop.

"No. Please. I don't want to."

I knew she was petrified. I could hear it in her voice. It always made my blood run cold.

"You know what will happen if you try to refuse me," he growled.

"But you promised. You said the other night was the last time."

"I lied," he answered with an evil tone.

I could hear her struggling with him, and her pleas pulled at me as she cried, "Please. Just stop."

I wrapped my fingers around the doorknob, my heart pounding in my chest as I eased the door open and stepped into her room. I found him, our guardian—the man who was supposed to love and protect us, holding her down on the bed. His pants were unbuckled, and it was clear he was hurting her. After losing my parents and sister, she'd become the only real family I had, and seeing what he was doing to her enraged me. I charged forward as I shouted, "Get the hell off her!"

With a surprised look in his eyes, he turned to face me. His shock quickly turned to fury as he pulled himself off of the bed and started towards me. Before I had a chance to react, his hand was at my throat, his fingers cutting off my air supply as he tightened his grip and spat, "You got some nerve coming in here again, boy."

Just as the real horror was about to begin, the nightmare ended.

Gasping, I sat up in bed, relieved to see that I was in my room … in my bed. I ran my hands over my face, trying to wipe away the remnants of the dream, but it still clung to me, unwilling to release its hold. For some sadistic reason, it wanted me to remember, forcing me to relive the hell I'd encountered during the years I'd spent in that foster home. It wasn't fucking fair. I was just a kid. I was supposed to be loved and protected, but all I'd found was pain and suffering. I hated those fucking people. I hated them with every fiber of my being for the things they'd done to us, especially that last night—the night that permanently marked me. *That night* I lost a piece of my soul, leaving me utterly broken, and since then, I'd never been the same and knew I'd never be again.

I was destined to live in the shadows, but thankfully, I wasn't destined to live there alone. After years of living in my own personal hell, I became a member of Satan's Fury and found a place where I truly belonged—a place where I would be accepted for who I was. My brothers could see the good inside of me, where I could only see darkness. My inner demons were constantly pulling at me, frantically trying to take control, and every day I fought to keep them at bay. But the fight was over. I'd just been voted in as the club's new enforcer, and those inner demons were about to take the reins.

SHADOW

It was after midnight, and Murphy and I were feeling pretty unsettled as we headed into Frazier—a part of Memphis that most people avoided, especially at this time of night. For us, it wasn't its history of crime, the dilapidated houses, or the graffiti-lined streets of this area that had us feeling uneasy. Hell, we were used to that. Instead, we were concerned about the call, Gus, our club's president, had gotten from two of our handlers. Apparently, they'd run into some trouble and needed our help, but before they could tell him what was going on, the line went dead. That didn't sit well with Gus. He was a man who prided himself on knowing what was going on at all times, especially when it came to *his* club. To make matters worse, it wasn't the first call he'd gotten over the past few weeks. In fact, there had been several. A couple of our boys had been jumped and robbed while others had come up missing altogether. That shit just didn't happen. Even though our runners didn't wear a patch, they were our guys, *under our protec-*

tion, and everyone knew it. Whoever was fucking with our boys knew what they were doing, and there would be hell to pay.

Murphy pulled up to the curb and killed his engine. After I did the same, he turned to me and said, "Let's go check it out."

Eager to see what the hell was going on, he got off his bike and started down the dark, abandoned alleyway. As the club's sergeant-at-arms, it was Murphy's job to ensure the safety and security of the club, and he took his role seriously. Knowing that two of the men under his watch might be in danger had him on edge. I followed him down the alley, and as we headed further into the thick of darkness, an eerie feeling had me reaching for my .45. Even though we were downtown, it was quiet—too quiet, and only the low hum of rap music could be heard as I pulled my gun out of its holster. Just as we reached the second dumpster, I saw them—Spencer and Mayfield. They were two of our best handlers, and they were both lying on the ground with bullets in their heads. "Fuck."

Murphy quickly turned, and as soon as he saw our boys on the ground, he roared, "Goddamn it!"

He rushed over to each of them, checking for any signs of life, but it was clear they were both gone. "Murph … we need to call Gus."

Knowing Gus was going to be on the warpath when he heard the news, Murphy sighed as he reached for his phone. I listened as he described what we'd found, and even though I was standing several feet away, I could hear Gus's reaction as his voice blared through the other end of the phone. Once they were done talking, Murphy put his burner back in his pocket and said, "Gus is sending

Gunner over with a couple of prospects to pick up our boys and clean up this mess."

I nodded, then started walking further down the alley. I had no idea what I was looking for, but I hoped to find something that might help us figure out who'd killed Spencer and Mayfield. I'd just made it over to Third Street when I saw Boon Franklin sitting in his car. He was one of those guys who was always into something, and when he saw me walking towards him, his face grew pale. In a blink of an eye, he'd started his engine and sped off. Clearly there was something up, so I walked back to Murphy and informed him, "I just saw Boon Franklin parked around the corner, and he took off as soon as he saw me."

"Boon Franklin? That's a name I haven't heard in a while. Who's he running with these days?"

"Not sure. Might be worth finding out because something tells me, one way or another, he's behind this."

Turns out I was right.

It hadn't taken Riggs long to track him down using his cell phone, and once they ran him down, he and Blaze brought him back to the holding room at the clubhouse. Gus left it up to me to find out everything I could about his involvement with Spencer and Mayfield's deaths. I stood in the corner smoking a cigarette as I watched him whimper and whine like a wounded animal. I'd been working him over for around four hours and he'd yet to talk, but I wasn't worried. I was just getting started. By the time I was done with him, he'd tell me exactly what I needed to know. Without moving from my spot, I growled, "I'm not a man who likes to repeat myself, Boon."

"Then, stop asking me about your boys because I don't know shit. I swear it."

I knew he was lying.

"I think you do," I told him as I tossed my cigarette to the floor and started towards him. Boon was a big guy, at least six foot four and three hundred pounds; he was playing the tough guy, but I knew he was about to break. It was written all over his face.

He grimaced when he noticed me getting closer. "I done told you, asshole. I didn't knock off your boys."

"Haven't you been listening?" I reached my hand into the bucket, and his swollen eyes widened with panic as he watched me pull the rag out of the water. "I never asked you if you killed them. I already know you did. I asked you *why*."

With that, I placed the towel across his face, and while he pleaded with me to stop, I reached down for the jumper cables. I tapped them together to check for an active spark before I placed each end on either side of his head. When I pressed them against the rag, a jolt of electricity surged through his temples, making his entire body grow rigid. After several seconds, I removed the cables, and his body fell completely limp. I lowered the rag from his face, and his eyes trained on mine as he watched me place it back in the bucket. My voice was low and firm as I asked, "Why'd you do it, Boon?"

I stood there staring at him for a brief second, but when he didn't answer, I reached for the rag again. After I placed it over his face, he started to thrash from side to side as he tried to break free from his restraints, but it was no use. He wasn't going anywhere. Ignoring his attempt to free himself, I reached for the cables again, but stopped when he cried, "I can't take this shit anymore! Jasper ordered the hit. He's been the one behind them all."

And there it was.

Jasper was a local thug who'd been trying to make a name for himself for years. He'd tried everything from pimping out second-rate prostitutes to starting up his own little drug ring out on the East Side. We all knew he was a piece of shit, but since he'd managed to stay out of our way, we left him alone. That was all about to change. I cocked my eyebrow as I looked down at Boon and calmly asked, "And why would he go and do that?"

"I don't know, man. I swear, I don't. I just know he's got something going down. He's paying big money for every one of your guys we take out," he rambled.

And the plot thickened.

I lowered the rag back into the bucket and watched as Boon's shoulders sagged with relief. The man had taken one hell of a beating. Knowing his life was hanging in the balance, he'd done his best to keep his mouth shut about his new connection with Jasper, but in the end, he was just like all the others—he sang like a canary. I left him bound to his chair as I stepped out of the room and went down the hall to find Gus. It was time to tell him what I'd uncovered. As I walked towards my president's office, I thought about how much my life had changed since the Culebras came knocking at our door.

We'd taken a real hit when they came after our territory. They'd chosen Memphis as their startup location for their new meth lab, hoping to distribute their product throughout the southern region by transporting it down the Mississippi River. When they'd first arrived, they'd made it their mission to wipe out any and all competition, and when they'd set their sights on Satan's Fury, they'd not only destroyed our diner and garage, but they'd also killed two of our brothers, Runt and Lowball. Runt was a good man, and an even better enforcer. His position in the club wasn't an easy one, but he'd faced adversity head-on, never letting anything get him down. We all knew he wouldn't be easily replaced. Unfortunately, the club was under attack, and after we'd learned that Terry Dillion, one of our drug runners, had been aiding the Culebras in their pursuit, we brought him in for questioning. We all knew he had information on the Culebras—information the club needed to take them down, and even though it would mean letting the darkness rise to the surface, I knew I had it in me to make Terry talk. Thankfully, I was right. In a matter of hours, I'd gotten him to provide us with the intel the club needed to bring the Culebras down. By doing so, I'd proven myself worthy as the club's new enforcer, and since then, I'd done everything in my power to live up to Runt's legacy

ALEX

I can still remember that first day when I'd come rushing into *Hallie's Books and More* to get out of the rain. I was just hoping to catch my breath and dry off, but from the second I walked through the door, I knew I'd stumbled upon something special. I took a step back to inhale that comforting scent of vanilla, then glanced around the room at all the different seating areas scattered amongst the many shelves of books. There were fresh flowers on the tables and beautiful watercolors hanging on the walls, which made the place feel inviting —like the owner actually wanted you to stay a while. I had no idea if that was her true intention, but that's exactly what I was planning to do as I removed my raincoat and started to look for a place to rest my aching feet. I headed towards the back of the store, relieved to find a small sitting area off to itself. Without even looking at the title, I grabbed a book off the shelf and went to sit down on the rustic sofa. I lowered my bag to the floor, and as soon as I sat down, my entire body melted into the soft cushions. Even in my frazzled state, I immediately started to relax. At first I thought it was just the calming ambiance of the store, but then I realized there was another reason.

I don't know how long I'd been sitting there pretending to read when I heard a lady's gentle voice say, "It's been a long time since I've seen anyone who was interested in the mystical words of Shelley."

Having no idea what she was talking about, I glanced up at the attractive, older woman with a look of confusion and asked, "Sorry. Words of who?"

A knowing smile spread across her face as she answered, "Mary Shelley. The author of *Frankenstein* ... The book you've been reading for the past hour."

I glanced down at the book in my hand and grimaced. "Oh, yeah. Of course. I just wasn't thinking."

"She's always been one of my all-time favorites." While I'd never laid eyes on her before, there was something familiar about her, making me feel instantly at ease. Her gray hair was pulled up into a loose bun, and she was wearing a long purple-and-white, tie-dyed hippie dress with open-toed sandals. She had a wrist full of bangles that jingled whenever she moved and eyes that were as blue as the ocean. "But then ... I have many favorites. My love for books is why I opened this bookstore."

"This is your place?"

"Has been since the day it opened twenty years ago. Granted, things have changed a lot since then, especially with all the bigger bookstores popping up on every corner."

"This place is amazing. Those chain stores can't begin to compare to yours. Not even close."

"You are sweet to say that, but lately my sales are telling me something different."

I could hear the disappointment in her voice, and I found myself wanting to help find a solution. Having no clue what I was talking about, I suggested, "You could always try buying and selling used books. That was a big thing back in my home town."

She cocked her eyebrow and replied, "Hmmm … You know, that's not a bad idea."

"You never know. It might be worth a try."

"I guess it's something to think about." She pondered the thought for a moment, then asked, "So, are you new in town? I don't think I've ever seen you around these parts before."

"Yes, ma'am. I just got here a few days ago."

"Well, welcome to Memphis. You need to be mindful of what part of town you're in. It isn't safe for a young lady traveling alone around here," she warned.

"I'll be careful," I assured her.

"Good." She lingered for just a moment before she said, "Well, I'll leave you to it. Everyone calls me Ms. Hallie. If you need anything, just let me know."

"Thanks, Ms. Hallie. I will."

An hour or so passed, and the store had grown quiet. I considered leaving, but for the first time in days, I actually felt at peace. I nestled back on the sofa and listened to the sound of the storm as I leaned my head back. It wasn't long before my eyelids grew heavy, and I found myself drifting off to sleep. After all the sleepless nights and the days spent driving, I was beyond exhausted, and it finally caught up with me. I probably would've slept through the night if she hadn't come over to wake me up. When I felt a tap on my leg, I sat up with a startled gasp. I looked up and was completely mortified to find the owner looking down at me with a worried expression. I quickly gathered my things and said, "I am so sorry. I can't believe I fell asleep like that."

"It's fine, dear. No need to apologize."

I jumped up off the sofa and started for the door. "You must think I'm some kind of a basket case."

"Not at all. I can't tell you how many times I've had a customer doze off. It just means that they felt comfortable enough to do so. I take it as a compliment."

"Well, thanks for understanding. Good night."

The door closed behind me, and I was immediately surrounded by darkness. I looked up and down the street in search of my car, but I was still feeling a bit dazed and couldn't remember where I'd parked. I was just starting to panic when the door creaked open and Ms. Hallie asked, "Is everything okay?"

"Yes, ma'am. I'm just trying to find my car." And then it hit me. I wasn't looking for the diamond-white BMW I'd driven for the past two years—the car that my father had given me on my sixteenth birthday. I'd traded it three states back for an older, four-door Nissan with a *Honk If You're Horny* sticker on the back bumper. As soon as the thought crossed my mind, I spotted my new prize parked across the street. I pointed to it and told her, "Oh, there it is!"

"Okay, dear. Drive safe."

She watched as I rushed across the street to get in my car. I could see her standing inside the door as I inserted my key and turned the ignition. She was still standing there when there was only a clicking sound as the engine refused to turn over. I tried over and over to get that stupid car to start, but the thing wouldn't budge. I knew I was in trouble. Ms. Hallie had warned me that this wasn't a good part of town, so I knew staying put wasn't an option. Just as I was starting to panic, I heard a tap on my window. I glanced up and found Ms. Hallie standing there. "Is everything okay?"

I didn't know what compelled her to come out and check on me, but I was so relieved that she did. I eased my door open and said, "My car won't start."

"I see that. Why don't you come inside? I have plenty of room at my place. You can stay with me. We can have someone come see about your car tomorrow."

"No. I couldn't put you out like that."

"Sure, you can. Besides, I'd love the company."

As great as her offer sounded, I wasn't sure what I should do. I had no idea who she was or why she was willing to help me. "I don't know."

"Honey, it's late, and if I had to guess, I'd say even if your car was running, you have no idea where you're headed."

"No. I don't guess I do."

"That's what I thought. Why don't you just take me up on my offer? I have a pot roast in the oven, and I'm gonna whip up a batch of mashed potatoes. I'd love for you to join me."

"That sounds so good. Are you sure you don't mind?"

"I'm positive. Now, grab your things and let's go get us a bite to eat."

"Okay."

I did as she said and grabbed my bag out of the back seat. Once I'd locked up the car, I followed her back into the store. As we headed upstairs to her apartment, she turned to me and asked, "Do you have a name?"

"Umm ... Yes, ma'am. I'm ... Alex. Alex Carpenter."

"Well, it's nice to meet you, Alex."

I never dreamed that I would find my sanctuary in a small book store in the middle of Memphis, Tennessee, but I did. Once Hallie realized that I didn't have a place of my own, she not only offered for me to stay with her, she insisted on it, and not only that, she gave me a job working at the bookstore. I don't know what I would've done without her. She knew I was running from something and was concerned for me. I could see it in her eyes whenever she looked at me, but she never asked questions. It was then that I realized why she seemed so familiar to me on the day we first met. She reminded me of my mother. They both loved unconditionally and with all of their hearts.

I wanted to tell her about my past, but I couldn't bring myself to say the words. Finding out the truth about my mother's death nearly destroyed me, and since the day I'd learned what really happened, I left home and never looked back. A part of me knew that running away wasn't the answer, but I felt trapped—imprisoned by the weight of the hatred I felt for the man who was responsible for taking my mother from me. I simply had no choice. I had to get the hell out of there, away from him—*my father*—and everything he represented, and save what was left of my sanity.

It had been almost eight years since the day I'd left home and found myself living with Hallie, my guardian angel. She showed me a life that I never knew was possible, a life filled with love and joy, and I absolutely adored her for it. During those times I'd spend listening to her stories, I felt safe in the world she'd created for us, like my past was just a distant memory. Hallie helped me see the endless possibilities of my future. Whether she realized it or not, she hadn't just given me a place to stay. She reminded me how it felt to have someone who truly cared about me, put *me* above others, and there was nothing in this world that could've felt better.

When Hallie died last year, I was completely heartbroken. She had been such a strong force in my life, and I had no idea what I would do without her. But in true Hallie fashion, she was always thinking one step ahead. Without even telling me, she'd left me the bookstore, along with the apartment upstairs. Even from the grave, she was looking out for me, and I was proud to continue her legacy.

Every morning, I woke up early and went downstairs to make a pot of coffee, water the plants, and dust the shelves. I'd learned from Hallie that presentation was everything, so I wanted to make sure that the store was perfect before I opened the doors. While I was rushing around, I found myself wondering if this would be one of those mornings that *he'd* be around—the unbelievably hot biker who made my knees tremble and breath quicken. I knew very little about him, just that he'd stop by the bookstore from time to time, and while it was obviously not his intention, his routine had sparked my curiosity. He'd enter the front door, and after a brief greeting, he'd make himself a cup of coffee and find his way to the back of the store. Once he'd picked out a book, he'd make his way over to the very sofa that I'd found to be so comforting on my first visit and sit there for a half hour or so, drinking his coffee and reading silently. When he was finished, he'd place his empty cup in the garbage and put his book back in its proper location, leaving no sign that he'd even stopped by for a visit. As he made his way to the front door, he'd place a twenty on the counter and bid me farewell.

At first, I found his little routine intriguing, especially with his peculiar behavior, but over time, I'd started to look forward to him showing up, and this morning was no different. As soon as I had everything ready to start the day, I went over to unlock the door. I quickly glanced out the window, and butterflies rose to my stomach when I spotted him getting off his Harley. I silently cursed myself for having such an instant reaction to a man who rarely even spoke to me. There were times when I'd try to strike up a conversation, but quickly realized that small talk wasn't my strong suit. I'd ask him random questions, hoping that it would trigger a lengthy response, but I never got much out of him other than one word answers. I didn't exactly mind it. With each answer, he'd reveal a little more about himself, making me curious to know even more. I unlocked the door, flipped over the *Open* sign, and rushed to the front counter, trying to look like I was busy working on an order. The minute he walked in, I glanced up and my throat suddenly became dry when I saw how good he looked in his tight-fitted t-shirt and faded jeans. His gorgeous eyes skirted over to me when I smiled and said, "Morning!"

With little expression, he replied, "Morning."

He walked over to the side table and made himself a cup of coffee. Once he was done, he glanced back over to me before making his way to his spot on the sofa. I let him be as he skimmed through his book of the day, and I tried to focus on the few customers who filtered in, answering their questions about a particular book or author. I tried my best to ignore him entirely, but every so often, I'd find myself sneaking peeks over in that corner. I just couldn't help myself. I knew so little about the man who spent his mornings with me, and he wasn't exactly forthcoming about why he was there. My mind was still drifting when he came up and tossed a twenty-dollar bill on the counter. I wasn't surprised by his actions. It was something he did every time he came into the store. Normally, I'd just leave it alone, but something compelled me to say, "You know … you don't have to do that."

My breath caught when he stopped and turned to look at me with those beautiful blue eyes. "And what if I want to?"

He was standing right in front of me, just a few feet away, and suddenly I couldn't form a complete thought. I'd been around handsome men before, plenty of them, but never had I been so close to a man like him—the kind who inspired romance writers in the thick of the night. My eyes dropped to his chiseled jaw and full lips, and all I could do was just stand there stammering like an idiot. To make matters worse, he shifted his stance so that the oscillating fan blew on him in just the right direction, sending his scent spiraling towards me. Damn. Why did I have to go and open my big mouth?

SHADOW

There were days when I'd feel everything, and then there were days I felt completely numb. Those were the days I liked best. I didn't want to *feel*. I wanted no pain. No regret. No misguided hope. Nothing at all. I'd spent years trying to find something that would help me do just that. I'd tried alcohol, drugs, women, and even therapy, but only because my commanding officer demanded it. I'd been imprisoned during my time in Afghanistan, and knowing what that shit can do to a man, he thought it would help with any issues I might have with PTSD. Unfortunately, that wasn't the case. The counselor tried everything he could to get through to me, but I just wasn't ready to deal with the shit-storm that was raging inside my head, and there was nothing he could do or say to change that.

I decided to ignore what was happening to me, hoping that eventually it would all just go away. That didn't happen. The dreams had gotten worse, and the dull ache in my chest only grew more intense. I was fighting a losing battle until I happened to stroll into a small bookstore on the corner of Broad and Second. The minute I'd walked through the door, an odd feeling washed over me, and I was taken back by the strange sensation as I'd stood there looking around. It was like I'd stepped into another world—a world where all my bitterness and regret no longer clung to me, and for just a moment, I could simply let go and *breathe.*

I don't know why it had such an effect on me, maybe it reminded me of my home—*my real home*—where I'd always felt safe and at peace and loved and protected. I hadn't felt that way since my family was taken from me. While the bookstore didn't give me that *exact* same feeling, it was close. It felt so comfortable, so easy. There was never any fuss. I'd walk in and make myself a cup of coffee, then grab a book and find my way over to the sofa in the back of the store. It was quiet, but not too quiet. As I flipped through the pages of my book, I would hear movement at the front of the store, people whispering as they picked out a book, or the sound of the register after a purchase, and it set me at ease. In the beginning, that feeling was what brought me back here, but everything changed the moment the bookstore's beautiful Latina owner, Alex Carpenter, caught my eye. Whereas in the past, I'd gone there looking for a place to take a breath and maybe find some possible insights to my fucked-up head, I'd suddenly found myself popping in regularly just to catch another glimpse of her.

Today was no different. After a long night of dealing with Boon, I needed a distraction, and like always, she'd done just that. For a few minutes, I was able to forget about all the bullshit and clear my head. Once I felt ready to start my day, I tossed my Styrofoam cup in the trash and carried my book back over to the shelf where I'd found it. I glanced down at the title—*A Guide to Healing: Finding Your Way Through PTSD*—and for a brief second, I actually considered buying the damn thing. While I knew I had some of the symptoms that were associated with PTSD, I wasn't sure the diagnosis actually fit. The years I'd spent in Afghanistan were unforgiving, especially considering the time I'd spent in captivity and the amount of bloodshed I'd seen, but nothing that happened there could even compare to the hell I went through in foster care. The torture, the endless beatings and mental abuse I'd experienced during those years were enough to scar any man. It was tough, but even that wasn't as devastating as losing the one person who actually understood what I was going through. My life was one fucking heartbreak after the next, but looking back, I realized those years molded me into the man I am today. Knowing there was no quick fix for the issues I had, I put the book back on the shelf next to the others. I walked up front where Alex was standing behind the counter, and she smiled as soon as she noticed me coming towards her. I gave her a quick nod as I placed a twenty-dollar bill on the counter and headed for the door.

Just before I walked out, she announced, "You know … you don't have to do that."

She rarely spoke to me, so her comment caught me off guard. "Do what?"

"Give me twenty dollars every time you come in. It's really not necessary. It's not like you ever buy anything, and the coffee is free for anyone who wants it."

While she might've found it unnecessary, I disagreed.

Every time I'd come in, I'd invaded her space, drank her coffee, and read one of her books without actually buying it. Giving her the money was the right thing to do. "And what if I want to?"

My rebuttal seemed to catch her off guard as her demeanor quickly changed. A look of panic washed over her as she stood there staring at me, and it took her several seconds to forge her response. She seemed almost flustered as she answered, "Oh, well … *if you want to* … that's fine. I mean … It's more than fine. I just didn't want you to think you had to do it, because *you don't*."

"Never did, but thanks for clarifying."

A light blush crept over her face as she smiled, and while it seemed innocent and sweet enough, I could tell there was some sadness hidden beneath it, which made me curious as to what had put it there. "Umm … Okay, then."

Her stunning, dark eyes locked on mine as I nodded, and just before I turned to leave, I repeated her words, "Okay, then."

"Hope to see you later," she called out in a timid voice.

I looked back over my shoulder. "*You will*."

I walked outside and over to my bike. After I hopped on, I threw on my helmet and glanced back over to the bookstore. I spotted Alex sitting at the counter with her head in her hands as she slowly shook it side to side, clearly rattled by our exchange. It was at *that* moment an odd feeling stirred in my gut, one I hadn't felt in longer than I could remember, and I almost, *almost* fucking smiled. Surprised by my reaction, I started my bike and pulled away from the curb, pushing back those unwanted feelings as I headed towards the clubhouse. It was time to see if Gus had been able to track down Jasper. Like me, my president was eager to find out exactly what was going on with Jasper and his new interest in our boys. When I pulled through the gate, Blaze and his son, Kevin, were outside talking to Riggs, and as soon as I parked my bike, Kevin rushed over to me with a big smile. "Did Dad tell you the news?"

Having no idea what he was talking about, I answered, "Not sure that he did."

"He's getting me a dirt bike!" he told me excitedly.

"A dirt bike? That's cool."

"It's awesome! He finally said I was old enough to have a bike of my own, and he said you might help me fix it up if we brought it over to the garage."

Along with being the enforcer, I also helped Blaze in the garage. While he mainly worked on remodeling vintage cars, I focused on classic motorcycles, bringing old, beatup bikes back to life. Thinking that a dirt bike would be a cool project, I nodded my head and said, "Yeah, I could do that."

"I knew you would help." He practically beamed as he announced, "It won't be long before I'll get a Harley and I can ride with you and the guys."

"Easy there, killer." Blaze chuckled. "Let's not get ahead of ourselves just yet. It's a dirt bike to use out at the farm."

"But it's a start."

"Yes, it is, and you're right—it'll be awesome," Riggs added.

Blaze patted him on the shoulder and said, "Why don't you run inside and grab your stuff. It's time for me to get you back to the house."

"Okay." Kevin started inside, but then quickly stopped and turned back to Blaze. "You did tell Gammy and Pop that you're getting me a dirt bike, right?"

"Not yet, but I will."

"*Dad,* you know she's gonna have a cow," Kevin whined.

"I'll handle your grandmother. You go get your things," Blaze assured him.

Once Kevin was gone, I looked over to Riggs and asked, "Moose have any luck finding Jasper?"

"Fuck no, and neither have I," Riggs grumbled. As the club's computer guru, if there was anything tech-wise that needed to be done, he was our man. There wasn't much the man *couldn't do*—from hacking into major government sites to locating people who'd done everything they could not to be found. The man was a fucking genius, and it was clear he wasn't happy that he hadn't been able to find our guy. "It's like the guy vanished into thin air."

"Okay then, bring me someone who'd know where he was. I'll get it out of them," I assured him.

"You sure Boon doesn't know?"

The mention of Boon's name brought an idea to my head. "No, but he might know someone who does."

"Worth a shot," Blaze added.

"Yes, it is." As I started to walk off, I looked to them both and said, "Let Gus know where I'll be."

"Headed that way now," Riggs replied.

As he made his way inside the clubhouse, Kevin came rushing out and yelled, "Yo, Dad! I'm ready to go!"

"It's about time. Get on the bike." Blaze nodded, then added, "I'll be right back."

Just as I entered the backside of the building, I heard

Blaze's motorcycle pull out of the gate, and from the sounds of it, he was eager to get Kevin to his grandparents' place. I took a few steps down the hall and entered the room where I'd left Boon. Smelling like something right out of the fucking sewer, he sat there bruised, swollen, and bound to the chair. With a pitiful expression, he looked up at me with pleading eyes and asked, "You gonna let me out of here or what?"

"Let you out of here? Now, why would I go and do that? We were just getting acquainted."

"Fuck, man," he groaned. "I've already told you everything I know. Just let me go."

I had to fight the urge to strangle him on the spot. Boon had killed two of our handlers, and if the fat fuck thought he was going to walk out of that room alive, he had another thing coming. But there was no sense in squashing his hope—at least not yet. I still needed information from him, and I didn't want to take the chance of him completely giving up on me. I crossed my arms as I looked down at him and said, "I have a few more questions for you."

"I'm done answering fucking questions, man." It had been eighteen hours or so since he'd experienced my handy work, so it wasn't a surprise that he needed a little reminding. I was running low on patience, so I decided not to waste any time and went straight for the jumper cables. As soon as I reached my hand into the bucket of water and grabbed the wet rag his breathing became strained, especially after I placed the rag over his face. All it took was the feeling of having that rag on his face to help him remember the pain he'd felt the day before, and he quickly changed his tune. "Alright! I'll tell you what you want to know!"

As I pulled the rag away from his face, I looked down at him and said, "Let's go back to Jasper. Tell me about the deal he made with you."

"He promised me five grand for each one of your boys I killed off. That's all I know."

"Five grand? That's a lot of money for a man like Jasper."

"I done told you that. I got no idea where he got his hands on that kind of cash, but he must be rolling in it now."

"What makes you say that?"

"So, about a week ago, he hired me to take out three of your other guys for the same amount of cash. It wasn't the kind of money I could pass up, so I told him I'd do it."

"And?"

"Well, I was right in the middle of taking care of them when someone came up. Even though I didn't get to finish the job, he still paid me a grand for roughing them up. Who the fuck does that?"

No one.

"Any idea where I can find him?"

"Jasper?" he asked with an overzealous shrug. "He's got his regular hangouts. That's where I always found him."

"And if he's not there?"

"Fuck, man. I got no idea."

"I need to know someone who would."

He thought for a moment, then said, "If Jasper was hiding out, there's only two people who'd know where he was. His right-hand man, Hoss, or Milton."

I'd known Hoss long before he started working with

Jasper. We'd crossed paths a time or two in the military, and he was quite the character. There wasn't anything the guy couldn't do, but he was mostly known for his storytelling. With his thick country accent and charismatic smile, he never had a problem drawing the attention of a crowd. He tried to make everyone think he was just a good old country boy, but I didn't buy it. The man was a trained killer, someone who was determined to get what he wanted, so I wasn't exactly surprised when I discovered he was working for Jasper. Milton, on the other hand, was a name I hadn't heard before. "Milton?"

"Yeah, that's his cousin … At least that's who he tells everyone he is. From what I've seen and heard they're pretty fucking close … like *too close for comfort* kind of fucking close."

I didn't need him to spell it out for me. "I got it. Any idea where I can find this Milton fella?"

"No idea, but I bet Hoss could tell ya. I'm sure he's been by his place with Jasper."

Boon had been helpful after all. I would take that into consideration when it was time to end him. Figuring I could do us both a favor, I walked over and grabbed the water hose, its drain was centered in the middle of the room. Runt had it installed to help with clean up, and over the last few weeks, I'd found it very useful. I flipped it on and pointed it in Boon's direction, attempting to wash his stench away. Once I was done, I released the chain that secured him to the floor and moved it over to the lock on the concrete wall, giving him a small amount of mobility. "I'll see what I can do about getting you some water and something to eat."

Trembling from the cold water that clung to his skin,

Boon looked over at the dirty cot like he'd just been given luxury accommodations. "Thanks, man."

He'd thanked me too soon. It was only a matter of time before the man who'd killed two of our men took his last breath. Boon had given me what I needed to find Jasper and had done so without turning it into hours of senseless torture. He'd earned a couple hours sleep and one last meal, but then, like anyone else who double-crossed Satan's Fury, he'd pay the ultimate price for his betrayal.

ALEX

When I first moved to Memphis, Hallie was the only friend I really had. It took some time for me to warm up to my new life, mainly because a big part of me knew it was only a matter of time before my past caught up with me. I was scared, but eventually, Hallie convinced me to take a chance—that living a life in the shadows wasn't really living. It was then that I finally started to venture out, and shortly afterwards, I ended up meeting my best friend, Jason. That day, I'd gone into the cutest little boutique to look for a Christmas gift for Hallie. As soon as I laid eyes on a snow globe with the Eiffel Tower in the center, I knew I'd found it. I rushed over to check out, and until then, I hadn't even noticed the guy standing behind the counter. He was tall, really tall, and slender with a smile that was filled with mischief. I knew immediately that there was something about him I was going to like.

"Hi. Did you find everything okay?"

"Yes. Thanks."

He took the snow globe off the counter, and as he gave it a quick shake, he asked, "Is this gonna be all?"

"Yes. That's it."

Still staring at the tiny white speckles that were floating around in the water, he said, "It'll be eighteen bucks."

I slid over a twenty. "Here ya go."

As he reached for the money, he looked over and studied me for a moment. "Do you go to State?"

I was ashamed to answer. "No. I guess you could say that I'm kind of new to the area. I thought about taking some classes this fall, but I'm not sure if I can work it out. You know how it can be."

"Oh, I totally get it." He ran his fingers through his dark hair and sighed. "I've about decided that school just isn't in the cards for me. I took a few classes in the spring, but flunked out. I guess I missed the memo where it said you actually have to go to class to pass."

"Yeah. That's where they get you." I giggled. "It's all just a sham."

"Exactly!" He laughed. "I'm Jason, by the way."

"Hi, Jason. I'm Alex."

"It's nice to meet ya, Alex."

Just as he was putting my gift in a bag, a young woman came out of the back room and walked over to us with a friendly smile. She stood beside Jason for a moment, and then gave him a nudge. "Since she's new to the area, you should invite her down to Newman's."

Jason rolled his eyes at her, then turned his attention back to me. As he handed me my change, he asked, "You ever been to Newman's?"

I shook my head. "Can't say that I have."

With a chuckle under his breath, he replied, "They have really great music. It's down on Sycamore. You should come check it out sometime."

"Oh, okay. I might just do that."

I'd barely gotten the words out of my mouth, when the young woman added, "We'll be there later tonight with a few friends. There's a new band coming into town, and word is they're pretty good."

"Sorry. This is my sister, Daphne. She can be pretty obnoxious about stuff," Jason sighed. "You might as well say you'll come; otherwise, she'll never let it go."

"Obnoxious? You're calling *me* obnoxious? You're the one who throws a tantrum whenever you miss *Westworld* or can't find your favorite lighter."

"Okay. *Pushy*."

"Well, I'm only pushy when I know I'm right," she answered defensively.

"Whatever."

She finally turned her attention back to me and asked, "So, can you make it?"

I studied the two of them as I tried to decide if they could be trusted, and then Jason gave me one of those smiles that made my doubts fade away. While I felt no attraction towards him whatsoever, he seemed like someone I would like to get to know. I was still a little apprehensive but answered, "Yeah, I think I can work it out."

"Great," she replied excitedly. "We'll save you a spot."

I left the boutique feeling excited about my plans for the evening, but by the time I made it back to the apartment, I started to have second thoughts. It had been so long since I'd had a friend my own age, and I was worried that I'd just end up making a fool of myself. Thankfully, at the time, Hallie was there to convince me that I was overthinking things and to put myself out there. She even helped me pick out an outfit and paid for my cab over to Newman's.

I was a nervous wreck when I walked inside, but as soon as I located Jason and made my way over to him and his friends, we immediately all started talking and laughing. They made me feel like I was one of their crew. It had been almost six years since that night, and from then on, we'd become the best of friends. I quickly learned that Jason and I had a great deal in common. Not only had his mother died several years earlier, he and his father weren't exactly on good terms. After spending several years in jail for embezzling from a local bank, his dad was never the same, and Jason did his best to steer clear of him. While I didn't tell him all the details of my past, he knew that I understood the pain he and his sister had gone through. When Hallie died, I don't know what I would've done without them. I'd probably still be in that apartment crying and wallowing in my heartbreak if they hadn't been there to help me get back on my feet.

Since one of my only two employees quit unexpectedly, I'd been spending most of my time at work, trying to pick up the slack. Jason had been on me for weeks to take a break, so I wasn't surprised when he called and said, "Newman's at nine."

Hearing the excitement in his voice, I replied, "What? Why? What's going on?"

"The Smoking Guns are in town!"

It had become Jason's mission to stay on top of all the new, upcoming bands that came through town, and we were usually right there beside him, making our own predictions about their future fate while we listened. It had become a tradition of sorts, so it wasn't unexpected when Jason called everyone in the crew to meet him down at the bar. "Wow. So, they're going to be at Newman's tonight?"

"Are you even listening to me?"

His voice was filled with frustration, and it was hard not to get tickled. "Yes, Jason. I'm listening, but you're really not telling me anything."

"I've said all you need to know," he snickered. "Get your ass down to Newman's at nine and wear something cool."

"Hold up … Just what exactly are you trying to say, numbnut?" I asked defensively. "I dress cool *all the time*."

"Umm ... No, you don't … But that's neither here nor there. Just dress to impress. It's the Smoking-*freaking*-Guns!"

If I didn't know him better, I might've been insulted by his comment, but I'd known Jason long enough to realize that he was just geared up over his favorite band playing in town. "Dang, you're really pumped about this band. I haven't seen you this excited since last year when the Backyard Dogs came into town."

"Don't get me wrong, the Smoking Guns are awesome, but they aren't the Backyard Dogs. They were incredible, and being there for their first music video was off-the-charts awesome."

Remembering that night, I added, "Yeah, that was pretty neat."

"*Neat?*" he scolded. "It wasn't just *neat,* Alex. It was amazing. I mean, how many times have you seen *Neptune* magazine come to Newman's for a band?"

"Okay. Okay. You're right. I've never seen anything like that, and it really was *a-maz-zing.*" I giggled.

"Hell yeah, it was."

"Well, who knows ... maybe the same thing will happen tonight with the Smoking Guns."

"A guy can hope, but I doubt it. They don't have the same kind of following." Jason sighed, then asked, "Anyway, do you want us to come and pick you up on our way over?"

Knowing he would want to stay until the very last song, I answered, "No, I'll meet you there."

"Suit yourself, just don't be late."

While some people were put off by Jason's strong personality, it was one of the reasons I enjoyed spending time with him. There was no guessing with him. He always said exactly what was on his mind and rarely held anything back. I found his outlook on life rather amusing. Whenever we were together, I'd spend the entire time laughing hysterically at something he'd said or done, and he had no clue why I'd found it so funny. At times, I'd find myself wondering why we hadn't tried the whole dating thing. He was handsome and smart, and he'd do anything in the world for me. But then, I'd remember there was absolutely no chemistry between us—like *none.* I'd be better off kissing a wet mop, so my sidekick, Jason, and I would forever remain in the friend zone, and I wouldn't have it any other way.

As soon as I walked in, I found Jason sitting at the bar talking to Daphne and her boyfriend, Jimmy. The minute he noticed me strolling towards them, he glanced down at his watch. "You're late."

I sighed and took a quick look over at the stage, where the band was still setting up. "Take a chill pill, dude. I'm like fifteen minutes late. Besides, they haven't even started playing."

"That's because they're not supposed to start for another half hour."

"Then, why did you tell me to be here at nine?"

"Cause, I figured you'd be late."

"I was late one time, and you're—"

"Babe, you're always late, but I've come to realize that it's just part of your charm." He glanced down at my fitted black-knit shirt and distressed jeans and smiled. "And I'm liking the duds."

I sat down next to him and replied, "Thanks. I'm glad you approve."

Daphne leaned forward and smiled. "Hey, Lex. You want something to drink?"

"Sure. I'll have a beer."

Jimmy motioned over to the bartender, who then placed my drink down in front of me. I'd just picked it up to take a sip when Jason turned to me with a concerned expression. "Don't forget you're driving."

Before I could respond, Daphne asked, "Hey, did I tell you about Jimmy's new job promotion?"

While Daphne caught me up with her latest news, Jason stared anxiously at the stage as the band finally finished setting up, and his eyes lit up when the lead singer stepped up to the microphone. The minute they finally started to play, Jason could barely contain himself, and I couldn't help but smile when his head started bobbing to the music. After they played a few songs, he leaned over to me and asked, "They're awesome, right?"

My eyes skirted over to the stage, and as I focused on the band's music, I just couldn't understand why he loved them like he did. Even though I knew it would drive him nuts, I shrugged and said, "I've heard better."

"*What?*"

"I mean ... they're okay, but I thought the Rickets were better."

"Oh, good grief. Why are we even friends?"

I smirked as I answered, "Because I'm the only one who will put up with your delightful personality, and you're the only one who will put up with mine."

"You got me there," he chuckled. "You wanna hit the Red Birds game next week? Some of the guys are getting a group together."

"Maybe. I'll let you know after I check the schedule at work."

He nodded, then turned his attention back to the stage. I sat and listened to the raucous stream of melodies for another hour, and when I couldn't take it anymore, I patted Jason on the shoulder. "I'm heading out."

"But they're not done."

"We have a big order coming in early tomorrow. I've got to be there to get everything sorted."

"Okay, but text me as soon as you get home."

I nodded, then went over to Daphne and Jimmy and said my goodbyes to them. It was after eleven when I headed out to the dimly-lit parking lot, and no one was in sight most likely due to the band still playing. I had an uneasy feeling and suddenly wished I was parked closer. I'd only taken a few steps when I heard the loud rumble of several motorcycles approaching, and as they got closer, I noticed something familiar about one of the men. Even in the pitch black of night, I knew it was *him*—the hot biker from the bookstore. I stood frozen in place as he and his friend whipped past me.

A black SUV pulled in right behind them as they all parked near the front door of Newman's. I watched in awe as he got off his motorcycle and removed his helmet. He turned to look in my direction, and as those penetrating blue eyes locked on mine, all my sense of reason seemed to just wash away. I couldn't move. My pulse was racing, my palms were sweating, and my hormones were raging. He looked so damn good with his dark hair tousled, and it was impossible not to notice how his jeans clung to him in all the right places. I was a complete mess. No man had ever had such an effect on me. I didn't like it. I wanted to get into my car and shake it off, but when I realized that he was leaving his two friends to walk in my direction, my mind and body just wouldn't cooperate. I simply stood there like a total idiot.

After he finally made his way over to me, I was surprised by his furrowed brow and intense expression. He just stood there staring at me for several seconds, and having no idea what else to do, I mumbled, "It's you."

"Yeah. It's me."

"I'm sorry … I don't actually know your name."

"It's Shadow." Before I could respond, he took a quick glance around the parking lot and asked, "You out here alone?"

"Yeah … I was just about to head home."

"You shouldn't be out here by yourself. It's not safe," he growled.

Surprised by his fierce tone, I became even more nervous and started to ramble. "I'm okay. My friends are inside. We were watching the band. I'm not sure if you've heard of them ... the Smoking Guns. They're pretty good. Not exactly my thing. A little loud for my taste. Not the loudest one I've ever been to, but close. At least I had an excuse to leave early ... I have a shipment coming in tomorrow morning, so I need to be at the store early. What about you? Are you here to see the band, too?"

"Not exactly." Without giving further explanation, he asked, "Where's your car?"

"Um ... it's right over there," I answered as I pointed in its direction.

He leaned to the side as he looked around me and grimaced, clearly not impressed by the state of my vehicle. "*That's* your car?"

"Yeah. I know it's not much, but it gets me to where I'm going."

Just when I thought the moment couldn't get any more uncomfortable, Jason stepped out of the bar, and as he glared at the burly biker standing next to me, he shouted, "Hey, Alex? You okay?"

"Yeah. I'm good. I was just about to leave." When he didn't move, I said, "You're going to miss the closer if you don't go back inside."

"You're sure you're okay?"

"Yes, Jason. I'm fine."

"Okay. Don't forget to text me when you get home."

"I will. Don't worry."

Once he was gone, I turned my attention back to my

biker. He studied me for a moment, his eyes lingering on my mouth for only a fleeting moment; then, without saying a word, he started walking towards my car. Having no idea what he was doing, I just stood there trying to wrap my head around exactly what was happening. He turned around and looked over at me then said, "I thought you were leaving."

"I am." He cocked his eyebrow as he motioned his hand towards the driver's side door. Feeling like a complete idiot, I rushed over to him and quickly unlocked my door.

He watched me get inside and asked, "You okay to drive?"

"Yes, I'm fine." He again stared at me for a moment like he was trying to decide if I really *was* okay. "Seriously. I had one beer two hours ago. I'm fine."

"Good."

I expected him to step back, but he just stood there looking down at me. I felt warm all over, my heart was pounding so loudly that I was certain he could hear it. I felt my face turning red, and not wanting him to see my body's reaction to him, I said, "Your motorcycle is really something. I bet it's awesome to ride on a night like this."

"It is."

"Okay, well … I guess I better get going." With a bit of hesitation, I put my hand on the door handle and as I started to close it, I said, "Thanks for walking me to my car."

His expression softened as he moved out of the way and said, "Be careful."

"I will. Thanks."

After I closed the door, I gave him a smile and a quick

wave goodbye, then started my engine. As I pulled out of the parking lot, I glanced up at my rearview mirror, and a chill ran down my spine when I noticed he was still standing in the same spot, watching intently as I drove out onto the main road.

"Damn," I muttered to myself.

SHADOW

Once I'd informed Gus about everything Boon had told me, he called everyone into church. Since our runners were under the gun, Gus made the call to up our watch on our boys. In hopes of deterring any further hits, he instructed us to have eyes on them any time they were on the streets. After assigning our rotations, he gave the order for Murphy, T-Bone, and me to bring in Hoss, hoping that he would lead us to Jasper. As soon as we were dismissed, Murphy and I headed out to our bikes while T-bone followed us in his SUV. We'd tried to track him down for over an hour when Murphy spotted his shiny, souped-up 2018 silver Chevrolet Dually parked by the front door of Newman's. With its lift kit and oversized tires, the damn thing was like a flashing neon sign, making him impossible *not* to be noticed. When we pulled into the front of the bar, the last thing I expected was to find the girl from the bookstore standing all alone in the parking lot.

Seeing Alex there was a distraction I didn't need. I

should've been focused on the task at hand, but the mere thought of something happening to her while she was out there all by herself had me coming unglued. The gut reaction confused me. At the moment nothing seemed as important as making certain she was safe. I wasn't sure why I was so driven. Actually, the feeling came as a shock to me, but I didn't hesitate. I just started towards her.

When I reached her, I noticed just how beautiful she looked. Her dark, thick hair fell softly around her face, and I was completely spellbound by her flawless olive skin and captivating dark eyes. Somehow, I gathered my wits enough to ask her if she was okay. Once I got her back to her car, I thought that would be the end of it—but I was wrong. As I stood there watching her tail lights fade into the darkness, I found myself longing for just one more moment with her. It was a feeling I wasn't accustomed to. Hell, I wasn't a man who *longed* for anything, and it was fucking with my head. I was lost in my thoughts when I heard, "Yo, Shadow. You coming or what?"

"Yeah. I'm coming."

As soon as I made my way over to them, Murphy asked, "She a friend of yours?"

"Not exactly."

"I don't know about that. She was looking pretty friendly to me." T-Bone snickered, but his smirk quickly faded when he noticed the expression on my face. "Hey, man. I was just saying."

As soon as we stepped inside, my brothers' interest in Alex was quickly forgotten, and their focus returned to finding Hoss. The band's music was blaring as we started shifting through the crowd, and as I listened to the lyrics,

I found myself thinking about what Alex had said. She was right. They were loud, obnoxiously so, and I was relieved when Murphy turned to us and yelled, "He's at the bar."

T-Bone and I followed him over to Hoss, and when he noticed that we'd come up behind him, he bowed his broad shoulders and gave us a smug look. With his country accent in full swing, he snickered. "Well, lookie here. It's the brothers of Satan's Fury. What brings you fellas down here? You checking out the band."

"Don't give a shit about the fucking band, Hoss." Murphy took a step towards him as he continued, "We came here looking for you."

"Well, how 'bout that. I'm honored. What can I do you fer?"

"You can tell us where we can find Jasper."

He inhaled a quick breath, and it was clear from his expression that the question had caught him by surprise. "Fuck if I know."

"Now, we both know that's not true," Murphy growled. "So, let's just skip the bullshit and tell us where he is."

He adjusted his ball cap and asked, "And why would I do that?"

"Cause you're going to be in for one hell of a night if you don't," T-Bone warned.

His eyes narrowed as he grumbled, "You threatening me?"

"You know us well enough to realize we don't make threats," Murphy barked. "So, I'm gonna ask you this one last time … Where the fuck is Jasper?"

He stood up and stuck out his chest as he replied,

"Well, I guess you're gonna have to make good on your fucking threat, cause I ain't gonna tell you shit."

Murphy gave T-Bone the nod and said, "Alright, then. Have it your way."

Even though Hoss was a fairly big guy, trained to handle situations just like these, he was no match for T-Bone. With one hard blow to the jaw, he had Hoss flailing backwards. He was trying to regain his footing when I reached out and grabbed the collar of his shirt. People started to scatter as I pulled him forward and slammed my knee into his gut. He hurled forward, clutching his stomach as he gasped for breath. Before he could regain his composure, Murphy grabbed his head and slammed it against the counter, knocking him unconscious. When he dropped to the floor like a two-ton weight, T-Bone looked over to me and said, "Let's haul this motherfucker to the truck and get the hell out of here. This fucking band is giving me a headache."

We got him restrained and loaded into T-Bone's SUV, then Murphy and I jumped on our bikes and followed T-Bone out onto the main road. Hoss was still out of sorts when we reached the clubhouse, but he could walk, which made it easier to get him down to the holding cell. Once we were inside, Hoss's eyes widened with panic. "What the fuck?"

"You ready to tell us where we can find Jasper?" Murphy asked as he shoved him further into the room.

While it was similar to the one where I'd worked on Boon, this room was bigger with a wider variety of restraints. Even though it was clear from his expression that he was freaked out, Hoss shook his head. "Fuck, no."

I reached for one of the chains that were mounted to

the wall, then fastened the cuff around his wrist. "I was hoping you'd say that."

T-Bone took the chain from the opposite wall and secured it to his other wrist, binding him into a standing position with his arms extended from his sides. He tugged at the restraints, trying with all his might to break free as he shouted, "You can't do this!"

With a gloating smirk, T-Bone relayed, "We already have."

"Let me out of here!"

"You tell us where we can find Jasper, and then we'll think about it."

"Fuck you!"

T-Bone lunged forward, punching Hoss square in the mouth and again in his gut. "You'd do good to remember who you're talking to, motherfucker."

Blood trickled from Hoss's bottom lip as he grumbled under his breath, "This is bullshit. I don't even know where Jasper is."

"We'll give you some time to remember," I told him as we started walking towards the door, but before I left the room, I turned the heat up as high as it would go. Since it was already sweltering outside, it wouldn't take long for the place to feel like a sweatbox. By morning, he'd be fighting heat exhaustion, and every muscle in his body would be screaming for a reprieve.

Once we were in the hall, Murphy turned to me and asked, "He's a stubborn one. You gonna be able to make him talk?"

"Yeah, he'll talk," I assured him.

"That's what I wanted to hear." As he started towards the front door, he ordered, "I'll let Gus know we got him.

You get your ass some sleep, brother. Something tells me you're gonna need it."

He wasn't wrong. I would definitely need to bring my A game in order to get the intel I needed from Hoss. So, I made myself a sandwich and had a hot shower, then fell asleep as soon as my head hit the pillow.

The next morning, I pulled my ass out of bed, got dressed, and headed out to my bike. Before I went to see about Hoss, I needed to make a run to the hardware store for a few necessities. I had all intentions of going straight there and back, but after I'd gotten everything I needed, I took a detour and wound up over at the bookstore.

As I rode up to the front of the store, there was a delivery truck pulling away from the curb, so it was no surprise when I walked in to find Alex sorting through several large boxes of books. Hearing the door close behind me, she looked up with a bright smile. "Morning, Shadow."

"Morning."

"Did you enjoy the band last night?" she asked as she bent down to pick up one of the boxes.

Before she could lift it, I stepped over and took it out of her hands. "Where do you want it?"

"Oh … um. Thanks." Then, she pointed to the front counter. "You can place it over there."

"What about the others?"

"Oh, you don't have to do that."

I cocked my eyebrow. "And if I want to?"

A light blush crept over her face as she smiled. "Well, then … it would be great if you could put them over on the counter, too. I should've had the delivery guy do it, but I just didn't think about it."

I picked up the next two boxes and carried them over to the counter as well. "This all of them?"

"Yes. That's it, and thanks. I really appreciate it."

I nodded, then ambled over to make myself a cup of coffee. Just as I was about to head to my spot in the back, I heard her say, "You never told me what you thought of the band last night."

"You were right. They weren't all that great."

"Yeah, I was really hoping they would be better. Do you go to Newman's very often?"

"Not if I can help it."

"Oh." She shrugged. "They usually have pretty good music. You should check them out sometimes. My friends and I hang out there all the time."

"Might just do that," I lied.

"Good deal. Oh, I umm … wanted to thank you again for making sure I got to my car okay last night. That was very thoughtful of you."

When I turned to reply, I found her standing right behind me. She looked so fucking cute in her oversized Def Leopard t-shirt and ripped jeans. Her hair was pulled up in a messy bun, and for the first time, I noticed that she had tiny freckles on the bridge of her nose. I had to fight the urge to reach for her. "Not a problem."

Standing close to her was fucking with my head, so I quickly turned and headed to the back of the store. After I'd grabbed a book, I sat down on the sofa and started reading. I could hear her up front sorting through the boxes, and something about knowing that she was preoccupied helped me to relax. By the time I finished my coffee, I was feeling recharged and ready to face the long day ahead. I was just about to put my book away when I heard a loud bang. It wasn't until that moment when I realized I hadn't heard Alex in several minutes, and as I made my way up front, I had an uneasy feeling after I saw no sign of her anywhere. That feeling was only made worse as soon as I heard a second loud thud coming from the alley entrance of the store. Concerned that something might be wrong, I rushed over to the back door, and when I eased it open, I found Alex cornered between the dumpster and the back of building. Two young thugs, wearing blue bandanas around their heads, stood in front of her, and when I noticed that one of them was sporting a knife, my blood ran cold.

Unlike me, Alex seemed unfazed by her perilous situation. Her voice was void of expression as she warned, "I'm going to say this one last time … back away."

The motherfucker with his pocketknife aimed at her throat, cocked his head to the side and asked, "And if we don't?"

Her voice remained eerily calm as she answered, "Trust me. You don't want to find out."

"Look at this stupid bitch trying to be all tough." The other one laughed, but when he saw me advancing towards them, his smile quickly faded. "Hey, man. We've got company."

"Let the girl go," I demanded as each of them turned to face me.

The punk with no weapon took a step back and mumbled, "Look man … we don't want no trouble."

"From where I'm standing, it looks like you've already found it."

I reached out and grabbed the kid holding the knife at Alex's throat, and as I slammed him against the wall, he cried, “We weren’t gonna hurt her. We was just trying to score a few bucks, man.”

“You’re about to score a whole lot more than that, asshole. Drop the knife. Now.” When the cheap metal hit the ground, his buddy took off running, leaving him alone to deal with the consequences of their actions.

“Please, man. Let me go.”

I tightened my grip on his throat, making it difficult for him to breathe, and he was growing limp when Alex put her hand on my shoulder. I turned to look at her, and she whispered softly, “Let him go.”

“I can’t do that.”

“Yes, you can.” Her expression lightened as she added, “I’m fine. He’s just some stupid kid who’s trying to be something he’s not.”

I loosened my hold on the kid’s neck, but before I let him go, I pulled him closer and said, “You show your face around here again, and you’re done.”

“Yes, sir.”

As soon as I released him, he darted down the alley like a bolt of lightning. Once he was gone I stepped towards Alex, who was looking up at me with those beautiful dark eyes, and I knew I was in trouble. My need to reach for her was almost too much to bear, and I was about to lose the last of my restraint when she moved in front of me and placed the palms of her hands on my chest. “You were pretty amazing.”

I inhaled a deep breath as my eyes dropped to her hand. I couldn’t remember the last time someone touched me, and it took me a moment to collect my thoughts. After several seconds, I finally managed to ask her, “You okay?”

"Yep. I'm all good."

"Have you had trouble with these guys before?"

"Well, *not them* … but there have been a couple of others. It's not a big deal. It just comes with the territory, but it's nothing I can't handle."

I took a quick glance around the deserted alleyway and wasn't happy when I noticed there were zero security lights and not a single camera in sight. To make matters worse, the locks on the backdoor were as old as the building itself. "You gotta step up your security."

She shrugged. I could hear a hint of embarrassment when she said, "I know. I just can't afford it right now."

Seeing that it was a sensitive subject, I motioned her towards the door. "Let's get you back inside."

"Okay."

I followed her back into the store, and as she was locking the door behind us, she turned to me and said, "I don't want you to get the wrong idea. The neighborhood isn't exactly the best, but there are lots of great people who live around here. Some have been really great customers."

"I get it, but that doesn't mean you don't need to be safe."

"You're right, but I've been doing okay." She gave me a half-smile as she continued, "I'll try to be more careful."

"If you ever get in a bind …"

Before I could finish my thought, my burner started to ring. I took it out of my pocket, and when I saw that it was Murphy calling, I quickly answered, "Yeah?"

"You in with Hoss?"

"Not yet. Had to take care of something."

"Does this something have to do with that chick from last night?"

"Not exactly."

"Um-hmm," he taunted. "I'll let you get back to it. Just let me know if you need a hand with Hoss."

"About to head that way now." After I hung up the phone, I turned to Alex and said, "I gotta get going."

"I kind of gathered that." She smiled and said, "But before you go I wanted to ask … would you like to come over for dinner tonight?"

My back stiffened. Her invitation caught me off guard, and my tone was almost harsh as I answered, "That's not a good idea."

"Why not? It would give me a chance to thank you for your help today … with the boxes and you know … those guys out back and all."

"That's not necessary."

"What if I want to?"

I was going to tell her no. The words were right there on the tip of my tongue, but then I looked into those beautiful dark eyes and I couldn't bring myself to say the words. "It'll be late before I could get here."

She grabbed a piece of paper, and after she wrote her number down, she handed it to me and said, "Doesn't matter what time. Just text me when you're on your way."

"Okay."

"Oh, and when you get here, just ring the buzzer outside the door. It's the one right next to the bookstore entrance. You can't miss it."

Even though I knew it was a bad idea to spend time with her alone, I nodded, then immediately turned and silently cursed myself as I walked out of the store. I needed to get a fucking grip before things got out of hand, but it wasn't going to be easy. I couldn't deny the fact that Alex had an effect on me, and it was my own damn fault. When I was around her, I let the memories of all those horrible nights of my childhood slip to the back of my mind. I didn't think about how I'd let my only friend down, how I hadn't been there in the way that she needed me to be. I managed to block out the sounds of her cries, the aching in my heart, and how my very soul was plagued with regret. I didn't think about the war, the countless explosions, the stench of death that lingered in the air, or the pain and starvation I'd endured while in captivity. All of those things were forgotten when she was close to me. Alex brought me out of the shadows, and even though I was being selfish, I wanted to remain there in the light with her. She deserved more than a man riddled with regret, a man who didn't know how to love or be loved, but I was helpless to resist her. Even though I'd tried to fight it, I'd let my guard down, and I wasn't sure I had it in me to put it back up. I wasn't sure I even wanted to. Damn. I was fucked. I jumped on my bike and started back towards the clubhouse, knowing exactly what I had to do. There was only one way I was going to get Alex Carpenter out of my head, and one way only. It was time for me to visit Hoss.

ALEX

After all these years, I could still remember my last training session with Marcus. It seemed like it was only yesterday when I was standing in front of him with the sweat beading across my brow while I waited for him to make his next move. For a man in his late forties, he was in exceptional shape. He had a toned, athletic build, and with his tall height and menacing, dark eyes, he could be quite intimidating when he wanted to be. Over the years, I'd learned a great deal about self-defense and him. Marcus wasn't a man who liked to lose, but after training for over an hour, I could tell from his sluggish movements that I was finally wearing him down. Man, how he hated that. He never once let me get the best of him, so it was only a matter of time before he tried to kick it up a notch. I figured he'd either come at me with a side kick, hoping to throw me off balance, or he'd advance with a combination of jabs and uppercuts, forcing me to shield the blows. While he always tried his best to keep me guessing, after years of working with him, I'd learned all his bags of tricks. I skirted over to his left, then back to his right, all the while taunting him with my overconfident smirk.

"You must remember … that a well-planned attack is fought with your mind, not your body," Marcus warned with a calm, yet stern voice.

"Um-hmm," I mumbled with an annoyed eye-roll. "You've mentioned that a time or two."

I'd barely gotten the words out of my mouth when he lunged forward and slipped his foot beneath mine, causing me to fall flat on my back. He stood over me with a disapproving scowl as he growled, "Then, maybe you should listen. It might keep you from ending up on your ass … or worse. *Dead*."

I pulled myself up into the sitting position and said, *"Dramatic much?"*

"It would do you good to drop the attitude." He extended his hand and helped me to my feet. "It's your life we're talking about."

"Yeah, but who's really gonna go to all this trouble just to get their hands on me?"

"Let's hope you never have to find out. Now, let's go again."

While there were times when he was overly intense and a bit overbearing, I knew he wanted to make sure I was prepared to handle anything that might come my way. At the time, I had no idea why he was so concerned. At eleven, I was simply too young to ask the right questions. I just knew that Marcus treated me like I was one of his own, like I was his own daughter, and I loved him for it—until I found out the truth, but that didn't happen until many years later. By then, he'd trained me to the best of his abilities, and he'd trained me well—very well. Even though that was a lifetime ago, I wasn't frightened when those two jerks showed up in the alley. In fact, I found myself hoping that one of them would try something stupid just so I could see if I still had the means to take them down. But before I had a chance to tap into my old skillsets, Shadow came charging out the backdoor.

The last thing I needed to do was draw unnecessary attention to myself, so I couldn't exactly let him see me take those guys down. I'd managed to keep my true identity a secret for seven years, and there was no reason to blow that now—especially after how hard I'd worked to keep anyone from finding out the truth. I knew it was a bad idea to even consider getting involved with someone, especially a man like Shadow. I knew nothing about him, *nothing at all.* I'd like to say that I was a good judge of character, but considering my past and how I always believed my father was someone he wasn't, I had no way of knowing if I could trust my gut instincts. Hell, for all I knew, he could've been a serial killer, a closet cross-dresser, or a sadomasochist asshole who preys on women in bookstores, and yet, I still invited him to dinner. The more I thought about it, the more I started to wonder if I'd made a huge mistake, and just as I was about to work myself into a tizzy, Jason walked into the store.

Without even saying hello, he gave me one of his looks and said, "What was up with you last night?"

"Nothing was up with me. Why?"

"I don't know. Maybe because you said you had to leave early because of work, but then I find you outside talking to a bunch of fucking bikers," he grumbled.

"I did have to work, and I wasn't talking to a bunch of bikers, Jason. I was talking to only *one*."

"Well, that's one too many, Alex."

Suddenly feeling defensive, I snapped, "What's that supposed to mean?"

"Those guys are bad news, Alex. They're into some bad shit. You should stay as far away from them as possible," he warned.

"Well, for somebody who's bad news, he was there to make sure I made it to my car safe and sound last night, and then, he helped me out this morning when two goons tried to give me a hard time."

His eyes widened as he hammered me with questions. "What the hell are you talking about? What two goons? Did anything happen? Are you okay?"

"I'm obviously fine, Jason, and it was no big deal. Just two young kids trying to act like they were tough, but Shadow ran them off."

"Shadow?" He grimaced. "The guy's name is Shadow? For fucks sake, Alex. Doesn't that tell you something right there? You're lucky you made it to your fucking car. God knows what this guy could've done."

"If you were so concerned, then why didn't you come out to help me last night?" I snapped.

"After the look you gave me? Are you kidding me?" he huffed. "It was pretty clear you didn't want me out there, but just so you know, I was watching from the window the entire time. I even had the bouncer waiting to step in if that asshole tried to pull something."

"Clearly, that wasn't necessary," I fussed. "Besides, I'm very capable of taking care of myself."

He crossed his arms and gave me one of his disapproving looks. "I've always thought so, but now I'm having my doubts."

"Well, stop with the doubts." Trying my best not to let him get to me, I walked around the counter and grabbed a handful of books. "And for what it's worth, even though I don't know him all that well, I happen to think Shadow is a nice guy."

His eyes narrowed as he asked, "So, what you're saying is, you've got a thing for this guy?"

"No, Jason," I said with exasperation. "I don't have a *thing* for this guy. I just think you're judging him too harshly, especially since you don't even know him!"

"I don't have to *know him, Alex*. I saw that he was wearing his patch last night. I know what it represents. Satan's Fury practically runs this city, and the fact we're talking about a place like Memphis and all the gangs we have in it, that's saying something. Hell, everybody knows they're into some pretty bad shit, and there's not a soul around who isn't afraid of these guys!"

"Okay. I've heard enough." While I didn't want to admit it, a part of me knew he was right. I heard all the rumors about Satan's Fury, and like Jason said, they weren't exactly good men. They were known for their violence and mayhem, and I could only imagine what Jason would say if he knew I'd invited one of them over for dinner. Hoping to keep that tidbit a secret, I started to make myself busy by organizing the books on the shelves as I declared, "I don't want to talk about this anymore."

"Why? Because you know I'm right?" he replied sarcastically.

"Because I think you're being a jerk!"

"You sure are getting defensive about some guy you

don't really know." He cocked his eyebrow. "You really *must* have a thing for him."

"Will you just stop already? You're going *way* overboard with all this."

"And why would you think I was going overboard?"

I turned to look at him and said, "I don't know, Jason. Why don't you tell me?"

"Because you're my best friend, and I'm worried about you!" He stepped towards me with a pained expression. "I don't know what I'd do if something happened to you."

The sincerity in his voice tugged at me, making me feel guilty for being so dismissive. "Nothing is going to happen to me, Jason, but if it makes you feel any better, I'll be careful. Okay?"

"And you'll steer clear of this Shadow guy?"

I hated lying to him, but I knew he wouldn't let it go unless I said—"I'll do my best."

"That's all I'm asking." He grabbed the rest of the books off the counter and brought them over to me. "Is this the last of it?"

"Yeah. That's it for now."

"Good. You wanna go get a burger or something?"

"I can't. Debbie called in sick, so it's just me today."

"You really need to hire some more help around here."

I couldn't say that he was wrong. I was working overtime after losing one of my best employees, and my other cashier, Debbie, wasn't exactly the most reliable person on the planet. I needed the help, but I simply didn't want to go through the hassle or the expense of hiring another employee. Seeing as I didn't want to get into another debate with him, I nodded. "I know and I will, but for now, I need to get back to work."

"Yeah, I guess I better do the same," he groaned as he headed for the door. "I'll catch up with you later."

Once he was gone, I made myself busy around the store, which wasn't exactly difficult since I was there alone. After I dealt with the few customers who came strolling in, I checked the time and realized I only had a half hour until closing time. I was suddenly overcome with nerves and excitement, and I was eager to get upstairs so I could start preparing dinner. I rushed around the place, picking up trash and putting away stray books, and when I got to the back of the store, I was surprised to see that Shadow's coffee cup and book were still sitting on the side table. With everything that had happened outside, he must've forgotten to put his things away, so I went over and placed the cup in the trash. I reached for the book he'd been reading and stopped dead in my tracks when I noticed the title—*Getting Past Your Past,* a New York Times bestselling book on how to deal with PTSD. I was beyond stunned, and as I stood there staring at that cover, I couldn't help but wonder why he'd chosen that particular genre. Was it just a fluke, or did he really have a traumatic past that he was trying to deal with?

That thought lingered in my head as I finished closing the store and headed upstairs. I was lost in my own thoughts as I searched the refrigerator and cabinets, looking for all the ingredients I'd need for Hallie's lasagna recipe. It was one of my all-time favorites and something that wouldn't be hard to warm up if he was late getting there. After I had everything prepared, I straightened up the apartment and headed for the shower. That's when it hit me. As I stood there trying to decide what to wear, my nerves started to set in and I couldn't stop thinking about everything that Jason had said. Then, I thought about the book he'd been reading and the fact that I really didn't know anything about him, and I started to wonder if maybe Jason had been right about everything. But then, I remembered the way he looked at me in Newman's parking lot and again in the alley behind the bookstore. That look was filled with enough intensity to melt the clothes right off of my body, and I couldn't deny it. I liked it. I liked it a lot. I'd only read about moments like that in romance novels, but I never expected it to happen to me, and just thinking about it brought butterflies to my stomach. Maybe I was wrong when I told Jason that I didn't have a thing for Shadow. Maybe I was very, very wrong.

SHADOW

When I got back to the clubhouse, I grabbed my recent purchase from the hardware store out of my saddlebag and headed to see Hoss. As I'd hoped, the minute I opened the door and saw him hanging there in the same position we'd left him, all my thoughts about Alex quickly disappeared. Just as it should be, my focus was solely on him and the information I needed him to divulge. I knew Gus and the rest of my brothers were counting on me, and there was no way I was going to let them down. When I stepped inside the room, the heat was so overwhelming that it was difficult to breathe, and the foul stench only made it worse. I looked over to Hoss and wasn't surprised to see that his clothes were soaked with sweat, and his wrists were bruised and bleeding from the long night of trying to keep himself upright. He was barely able to keep his eyes open as he swayed back, letting the chains pull taut as they kept him from falling. The guy was barely hanging on, and I hadn't even touched him.

I walked over to the corner of the room and grabbed an old wooden chair with a wicker seat. I placed it behind him, then walked over to the wall and loosened one of his restraints just enough for him to sit. With a pain-filled groan, he collapsed into the chair and his entire body went limp. I stepped over to him and snickered. "Morning, Hoss. You have a good night?"

His voice was weak and barely coherent, but he managed to reply, "Fuck you, asshole."

"I'll take that as a no." I opened a bottle of water and took a long drag before extending it out in front of his face. "You thirsty?"

Sweat trickled down from his brow as he pleaded, "Please!"

I shook the bottle above his head, and when he opened his mouth, I poured several drops over his tongue—just enough to make him desperate for more. "There's plenty more … You want it? All you have to do is tell me where I can find Jasper."

"Can't tell you that."

His eyes locked on the water bottle as I brought it up to my mouth and took another drink. "And why is that?"

"Cause if I talk, I'm as good as dead."

"What makes you think you're not already?" I motioned my hands around the room as I continued, "I mean, come on, man. From the looks of things, you're chances of getting out of here alive are pretty fucking slim."

"I'd rather take my chances here."

"Is that so?"

"Absolutely."

"I gotta say … that takes balls, Hoss." I walked over to

the wall and pulled on the chain connected to his wrist, forcing him back into a standing position. "Not exactly smart, but it takes balls."

I spent the next several hours trying an assortment of strategies to get him to talk, but he refused. I wasn't surprised. Like me, he'd been trained to keep his mouth shut, but my patience was wearing thin. I had plans that I wanted to keep, so I decided it was time to take it to the next level. I had something special planned for him, something that might just make him reconsider his stance on keeping quiet. His eyes were damn near swollen shut and his entire body was covered in bruises and blood as he watched me remove my pocketknife from my back pocket. When I reached for the chair and started cutting out the wicker seating, he asked, "What are you doing?"

I continued to cut away at the seat, making a large oval hole, much like a toilet seat, as I explained, "You know … there's a lot of interesting things about the Dutch. Dutch men are among the tallest in the world, they are the largest beer exporter, and the largest black licorice consumer on the planet. Amsterdam was built on poles, and they serve mayonnaise with their French fries. Crazy, right?"

"What the fuck are you talking about?"

"I'm talking about the Dutch, Hoss. Haven't you been listening?" I tossed the remains of the seat on the floor, then slid the chair back into its previous position behind Hoss. Once I had everything ready, I reached for my phone and sent a text message to Gus, requesting the assistance of a couple of prospects. "The Dutch are also famous for a particular technique they've acquired for extracting information."

His eyes widened as he tugged at his restraints, trying once again to break free. "What the hell are you talking about?"

Before I had a chance to answer, two of our newest prospects came into the room and got Hoss settled in the chair. Once they were gone, I walked over and grabbed my latest purchase off of the table: a long rope with an eight-pound weight attached to the end of it, and let it swing slowly at my side. "I'm not gonna lie to you. This here, Hoss? This shit is gonna hurt."

With pure horror in his eyes, he shrieked, "What are you gonna do?"

It didn't take long for him to find out the answer to that question, and in no time at all, he started running his chops, telling me what he knew about Jasper and his whereabouts. With his head hanging low, he muttered, "The last I heard, he was hiding out in some warehouse downtown."

"Why he's hiding?"

"Figure he's gotten in over his head."

"Gonna need more than that."

"You know Jasper's always done alright for himself, but he's never made it big. Now, all the sudden, he's spending all this dough to get your dealers off the streets. You ain't gotta be the sharpest tool in the shed to know he didn't come up with that idea or the money on his own."

"Then, whose money is it?"

"Fuck if I know. Just know this guy must be the real fucking deal. Jasper paid Tibbs to take care of one of your guys, and when he failed to follow through, Tibbs ended up gutted ... and I mean gutted like a goddamn deer, man. It was all kinds of fucked up. Jasper ain't got the balls for that shit, but this guy … whoever he is, he don't take shit off nobody and has the kind of money to make things happen."

"Where do you fit into all this?"

"That's just it. I don't. Jasper fucking cut me off. Said he didn't need my services anymore, which wasn't no sweat off my back. Figure I don't need that kind of hassle, but fuck, I know I'm just living on borrowed time."

"You know too much."

"Damn straight," he sighed. "It's only a matter of time before they try to end me, too."

Hearing that made it easier to understand why Hoss was so hesitant to break his silence. He didn't want to give them any more reasons for coming after him. "Gonna need to know which warehouse, Hoss."

He paused for a moment, then replied, "If there's anyone who knows the answer to that, it's gonna be Milton."

"His cousin?"

"Yeah, if *that's* what you wanna call him," Hoss scoffed. "Milton is a deranged motherfucker, man. He seems like a flaming homo and all that shit, and from what I can tell he is, but there's another side to him. That fucker is crazy as shit. Just as soon slit your throat and shove your dick down it than take any shit off ya, and not to knock what you got going here, but that psycho would just a soon die as to run his mouth on Jasper. If it was me … I'd save myself some time and just put eyes on him. It won't be no time before he'll lead you to Jasper."

With that, I headed towards the door. Right before I walked out, Hoss shouted, "Hey, man! You gonna leave me here like this?"

I turned and looked at him in his exposed state and simply shook my head as I headed out the door, slamming it behind me. Hoss wasn't going anywhere until we found Jasper. On my way down to Gus's office, I checked the time and saw that it was already after seven. Alex was waiting for me, and I could almost picture her in that little apartment making a nice dinner for the two of us. I'd never had anyone do anything like that for me, and even though it was wrong, I found myself looking forward to seeing her, to feeling that sense of ease whenever she was around—especially after my long day with Hoss.

I knocked on Gus's door, and once he'd given me the go ahead, I stepped inside. He looked up at me with a fierce expression and asked, "Got any news?"

"Got a lead on Jasper."

"Good. Whatcha got?"

"We need to get eyes on his cousin, Milton. He's our key to finding him."

He crossed his arms as he leaned back in his chair. "You're telling me that his right hand man didn't know where to find him?"

After I shared everything Hoss had told me, I said, "I can get him to talk," I assured him.

He nodded. "I have no doubt about that, son. None whatsoever."

"Then, it's your call. We can bring Milton in, or we put eyes on him."

"If what Hoss said is true, we'd save us all some time and trouble by just putting eyes on him." He reached for his phone as he said, "I'll get Riggs and Murphy on it now."

"Let me know when they find him. I'm heading out for a couple of hours, but I'll be close if you need me."

"Will do."

With a quick nod I turned to leave, satisfied that my president knew if the time came when he or the others needed me, I'd be there. As I headed to my room, I reached in my back pocket for Alex's number, then sent her a message, letting her know I'd be there in half an hour. Once she'd replied, I took a shower and threw on some fresh clothes. After I pulled on my boots, I headed out to my bike and cranked the engine, hoping that the ride over would help clear my head. While it did to some extent, I still felt a heaviness weighing down on me when I pulled up to her curb. At first I thought it was everything that was going on with the club, but as I started towards her door, it hit me. The weight I felt pressing down on my chest was my fucking nerves, and it took me by complete surprise. Over the years, I'd felt a wide assortment of feelings: mostly anger, resentment, hatred, and regret, but nervousness was an emotion that I hadn't felt since I was a kid. I didn't like it—not one fucking bit. I tried my best to pull my shit together, then I rang the buzzer like she'd told me; seconds later, I heard her footsteps coming down the stairs. The door eased open, and the mere sight her nearly took my breath. She looked absolutely stunning. Her long, dark hair was down around her shoulders, and she was wearing a pair of cutoff denim shorts with a fitted, dark-colored, V-neck t-shirt.

With a welcoming smile, she said, "You made it!"

"Sorry, it's so late."

"Don't be silly. You aren't late at all." Then, she motioned for me to follow. "Come on up."

I followed her up the stairs and couldn't help but notice that just like the store, there was little to protect her from the outside world. The locks on the front door were much like the back—old and damn near useless, and the lights in the exterior hall were dim, making it difficult to see. As we reached her apartment door, I was disappointed to find that the doorknob was loose, and there was no sign of a deadbolt of any kind. My need to protect this woman I barely knew seemed odd to me, but nonetheless the feeling was there. She eased the door open, and the delicious scent of Italian food made my stomach start to rumble from hunger. I followed her inside and was surprised to see how big her place was. It was an open studio apartment with exposed brick on the walls and large beams and pipes sprawled across the ceiling. While it hadn't been updated, it was much like the bookstore downstairs and had a very comfortable feeling to it. As I glanced around the room, I noticed it had all the necessities—a living room in one corner with an oversized sofa and chair, and a large kitchen right next to it. The dark cherry cabinets were tall, almost reaching the ceiling, and even though the appliances were dated, they added a bit of charm to the place. In the back corner, there was a small wall that offered little, but just enough, privacy to her bedroom. I knew studio apartments like this ran pretty steep in a city like Memphis, and with her only income coming from the bookstore, I couldn't help but wonder how she could afford it. Regardless, it suited her, and as I watched her walk into the kitchen, I told her, "Nice place."

She took a large bowl out of the refrigerator and replied, "Thank you. My … uh … grandmother left the apartment and the bookstore to me when she died last year."

"Hallie ... *Bookstore Hallie* was your grandmother?"

Suddenly, a strange look crossed her face. "Yes. At least in every way that counts, she was."

"I always thought a lot of her."

"You knew Hallie?"

"Yeah. We crossed paths a time or two. She was one of those rare people who didn't judge a book by its cover."

She smiled. "No, she didn't. She gave everybody a chance and always managed to find something good about everyone she met."

"Even us bikers."

"Yes. Even bikers," she giggled.

I walked over to her and asked, "Need a hand?"

"Umm ... You could put some ice in the glasses. They're in the cabinet beside the sink, on the left, and the sweet tea is in the fridge. I also have a beer or two in there if you'd rather have that."

I nodded, then headed over to the cabinet for the glasses. As I made our drinks, she went over to the stove and pulled out a large pan of lasagna and garlic toast. I leaned towards the food to get a better glimpse. "Looks good."

"Hopefully, it'll taste as good as it looks."

After she'd fixed us both a plate, I helped her bring everything over to the table, and once we were settled, we both started eating. Neither of us spoke, but the silence didn't bother me. It was something I'd become accustomed to. She, on the other hand, wasn't. I could tell by the way she was fidgeting that she was feeling uncomfortable, which started to make me feel the same way right along with her. I wanted to be normal for her, to be the kind of man that she deserved, but I knew that just wasn't possible. I wasn't that man, and even if I could change, I simply didn't know how. I would need help to change, and unbeknownst to me, I was about to get my first and most memorable lesson. After taking a sip of her tea, she shifted in her seat and asked, "So, what made you decide that you wanted to join Satan's Fury? Was it just because of the motorcycles, or did you like the idea of being part of a gang?"

"Satan's Fury isn't a gang. It's a club."

Clearly unnerved by my response, she started to ramble. "I'm sorry. I didn't mean anything by the gang comment. I don't really know much about motorcycle clubs and what they're all about. I'm sure there are lots of differences between you and all those gangs that are around here."

"I guess some would say we have our similarities, but we consider ourselves family and we give *our all* to the club, even if that means putting our lives on the line."

Her eyebrows furrowed. "Hmm ... *Lives on the line*? So, I guess some of the stories I've heard about Satan's Fury are true."

"Depends on what you've heard."

"That's a vague response."

I shrugged. "I'll tell you this ... As a member of the club, I always know my brothers have my back, no matter what the circumstance."

"I guess that would be kind of nice. Hallie was always that for me. There was nothing she wouldn't do for me, and I really miss having that. I have Jason and his sister, Daphne, but it just isn't the same."

My back stiffened at the sound of Jason's name. I'd never considered the fact that Alex might have a boyfriend, and while the feeling might've been irrational, the thought of her in another man's arms annoyed the hell out of me. I tried to keep my cool as I asked, "Jason?"

"Oh … where do I start?" A smile spread across her face as she continued, "Jason and I met a year or so after I moved here, and I guess we just kind of hit it off. We started hanging out, and it wasn't long before we were together all the time."

It wasn't exactly what I wanted to hear, but seeing that he made her happy made it somewhat easier to bear. "You seem to care a lot about him."

"Definitely. He means the world to me. When Hallie passed, he never left my side … I don't know what I would've done without him."

"So, you two have been together for a while?"

"What? Wait … No!" She shook her head feverishly. "Jason and I aren't together. He's just my friend … *a really good friend*, but that's it. Nothing more. Besides, I wouldn't have invited you to dinner if ..."

Her voice trailed off, and her cheeks suddenly turned a bright shade of pink. She'd just revealed something to me, but it took me a moment to realize exactly what she was saying. Damn. The dinner was more than just a way for her to thank me—much, much more. Feeling relieved by her confession, I replied, "Good to know."

ALEX

Sitting across the table from me, Shadow looked like every fantasy I'd ever had wrapped into one incredibly sexy package, and even though I tried my best to hide it, he was making me a nervous wreck. I knew a man as good-looking as Shadow could have any woman he wanted, and even though I tried to tell myself that he was just a man—no different than any other—I knew that wasn't true. Shadow was a strong, enigmatic force with a ferocity that couldn't be denied, and at times, he could be more than a little intimidating. That alone should've had me running for the hills, yet it was the last thing I wanted to do. Instead, I longed to touch him, feel his strength beneath my fingertips, and completely submit to my attraction to him. But there was something else I wanted even more. I wanted to get to know the man behind the walls he kept so guarded.

Hoping to gain a little insight to the man behind the leather, I said, "I've noticed that you stop by the bookstore quite often. Have you always been a big reader?"

"I guess you could say that." He glanced up at me as he continued, "I picked it up when I was younger. And you?"

"It came later for me. I guess you could say that Hallie rubbed off on me." I giggled. "She had me read a few of her favorites, and after that, I was hooked. There's nothing like the escape you can get from a good book."

"Yeah, I know what you mean."

"What is your favorite genre?"

"When I was younger, I was all about mystery and suspense, but now, I'll read just about anything." He took another bite of his lasagna before saying, "I like to get different perspectives on things. You know?"

Remembering the book he'd left on the table, I answered, "I do. I totally get it."

"Who knows? I might actually learn something from some crazy author one day."

"You never know." Hoping I wasn't crossing some imaginary line, I asked, "When did you join Satan's Fury?"

"A while ago … right after I got back from Afghanistan."

"Afghanistan? I didn't realize you had been in the military."

"It was a long time ago."

I couldn't help but wonder if his time at war was the reason why he'd been reading a book about PTSD. I wanted to ask him more about it, but it was clear from his tone that he didn't want to talk about it. Deciding to go another route, I asked, "What about your family? Are you close?"

"My parents and sister died in a house fire when I was ten."

"Oh, God. I'm so sorry. I can't imagine how hard that must've been for you."

"It was tough, but I got through it." His tone was lightened as he said, "My brothers are my family now."

"I'm glad you found them, especially after all you've been through."

"One of the best things that ever happened to me." He took another bite of his garlic bread before turning his focus back to me. "What about you? You close to your folks?"

"Hmm … not exactly." I was walking on shaky ground. I didn't want to lie straight out so I decided to be vague with my response. "My mother died a few years ago, and since then, my father and I have kind of lost touch."

"Sounds like you've had a pretty rough go of it, too."

"I guess we all have our crosses to bear, but like you, I got through it."

"Yeah, I'd say you were doing pretty well."

"I wouldn't go that far." I chuckled. "It's not always easy being on your own."

"But, you've got Jason," he teased.

I shook my head and smiled. "Yes. I do have him, and his sister, Daphne."

Since we'd both finished eating, I stood up and took our plates over to the sink. I was just about to turn around when he came up behind me with the rest of the dishes. He set them down on the counter next to me and said, "You're a good cook."

"Not really." I shrugged. "I was just following Hallie's recipe. She was the cook."

"Either way, dinner was delicious."

I looked over at him and smiled. "I'm glad you enjoyed it. Can I get you some more tea or maybe a beer?"

He ran his hand over his stomach and *almost* chuckled. "No, thanks. I'm good."

As soon as I finished putting the leftovers in the fridge, I started to feel anxious. I hadn't had many experiences with men. In fact, I'd only been intimate with two men in my life, both of which were a long time ago—*too long ago*. I'd all but forgotten how to show a man that I was interested in him, which only made matters worse because I was definitely interested in Shadow. While I knew it was impossible for me to have a real relationship with him, I still found myself drawn to him. I'd been attracted to him since the first day he'd walked into my bookstore, and here he was, just a few feet away. I finally had my chance to get closer to him, and I couldn't just let the opportunity pass me by. "Would you like to sit and talk for a while?"

"It's getting late. I should probably get going."

His answer was short and to the point, making me feel rejected. "Oh ... Okay."

Apparently, I hadn't done a good job of hiding my disappointment, because the next thing I knew, he was standing right in front of me with an intense expression on his face. His voice was low and strained as he whispered, "*Alex.*"

"Umm-hmm?"

"I want to stay. Hell, there's nothing in this world I'd rather do, but ... I just can't do it."

"But why? Is something wrong?"

"No, everything's good. That's the problem." His eyes locked on mine, and I felt a chill run down my spine as he continued, "I'm broken in ways you can't begin to imagine, Alex. You can do so much better than—"

Before he could finish his sentence, I placed the palms of my hands on his chest as I lifted up on my tiptoes and pressed my mouth against his, silencing him with a kiss. I felt his muscles stiffen and feared he'd push me away, but he didn't. Instead, he kissed me back. His lips were soft and warm, but his entire body was rigid and tense, letting me know that he was still having doubts. I'd heard what he was trying to say. I knew he was worried about being good enough, but I wanted him to forget about his concerns and become lost in the moment with me. I got my wish when I provoked him by slowly brushing my tongue against his bottom lip. His hand dove into my hair, his fingers clutching the nape of my neck as he pulled me closer. A low, needful groan vibrated through his chest as he delved deeper into my mouth, and it was all I could to do keep my footing as a wave of indescribable desire crashed over me. I'd never wanted a man like I wanted Shadow at that moment. I thought he was feeling the same, but just as I inched closer, he took a step back and pulled himself free from our embrace.

With his jaw clenched, he looked down at me and growled, "Baby, you really shouldn't have done that."

"What? Why?"

"Now that I've had a taste of you, all I'm gonna want is more … much, much … *more*."

Feeling brazen, I looked him straight in the eye and replied, "And what if I want *more*, too?"

Before I'd even had a chance to blink, he had me pinned against the wall, towering over me like a starved animal about to devour its last meal. Damn, he looked so unbelievably sexy as he hovered over me, and every single nerve in my body came alive as I watched him slowly lower his mouth to mine. The man who'd invaded my dreams for months kissed me long and hard, making me lose all my self-control. I let my fingers trail along the curves of his ever-so-defined chest and relished in the sensation of having him so close. Shadow felt perfect, like his body was made just for me, and I wanted to explore every inch of him. I was so caught up in the moment, I wasn't even thinking as my hand continued down towards his abdomen. When the tips of my fingers reached his belt buckle, he reached for my hand, stopping me dead in my tracks.

Shadow lowered his mouth to my ear and whispered, "You sure about this?"

"Absolutely."

With that, he kissed me again, and from the moment his lips touched mine, I knew he was done holding back. Like a man possessed, his hands became rough and impatient as they roamed over my body, and any doubts I'd had about my lack of experience disappeared. He took both my breasts in his hands, caressing each one through the thin fabric of my t-shirt. The way Shadow touched me made me feel so wanted, so utterly desirable—I couldn't get enough.

The warmth of his breath caressed my skin as he spoke in a hushed tone, "You have no idea what you do to me."

My heart raced as his hand inched its way down my stomach and slipped under the waistband of my shorts. When his fingers drifted lower, in between my legs, that was it. My entire body shivered with anticipation as the tips of his fingers grazed the lining of my lace panties. I loved the feeling of his hands on my body. Every single touch was like adding fuel to the fire, making me yearn for more. I rested my head on his shoulder and closed my eyes, relishing the sensation as he moved his fingers in slow, methodical circles against my clit. As soon as I started to feel that familiar tingling in my abdomen, he eased my panties to the side, and I had no doubt that he'd find I was already wet as his fingers easily slid deep inside me. While gently caressing my g-spot, he began teasing my clit with the pad of his thumb, using just the right amount of pressure to make me come unglued. It felt incredible, better than I'd ever dreamed possible, and after just a few moments, I felt my orgasm start to take hold. His fingers curled deep inside me, and when he increased the pressure on my clit, I was done. With a satisfied moan, my head fell back and my entire body started to tremble uncontrollably. My climax surged through me with a powerful force, causing me to mumble over and over, "Oh, God! Oh, God!"

I was practically floating, but my blissful haze quickly turned to disappointment as I felt him remove his hand from my panties. My eyes met his, and I nearly came again when he said, "I want to take this slow … but I can't. Not this time. Right now, I need to be inside you. I need to fuck you, long and hard. You okay with that?"

"I'm more than okay with that. I want you, Shadow." My hands dropped to his waist, and in a frenzy, I started to unbuckle his belt.

He reached into his back pocket and took out a condom. While I watched him ease it down over his long, thick shaft, I quickly removed my shorts and panties.

Once he was done, he lifted me up and pressed my back against the living room wall as I wrapped my legs around his waist, grazing his cock against my center. I simply couldn't wait a moment longer to have him inside me, so I reached between us and took his shaft in my hand, positioning him at my entrance. He lifted me up, then thrust deep inside of me in one fell swoop, and I gasped at the invasion. Concern flashed through his eyes as he asked, "You okay?"

I nodded as I mumbled, "Um-hmm. Please, don't stop."

He gave me a moment to adjust to him before he placed his hands on my hips and started to move, slow and easy. I tightened my legs around him, nudging him close to take him deeper. After Shadow took the cue, he pulled back and plunged into me, again and again, and it didn't take him long to find *that* spot which made every nerve tingle. Consumed with lust and emotion, I rocked my hips in time with his, meeting his every thrust, and with each second that passed, I was getting closer to the edge. He continued driving into me with the relentless rhythm he'd set, and it wasn't long before I felt my climax building, burning through my veins.

A deep groan resonated through his chest as he quickened his pace, and that was all it took. My release crashed over me, causing my entire body to tense around him. While still planted deep inside of me, he started towards the corner of the room and lowered me onto the sofa. Once I was settled, he reached for the hem of my t-shirt and pulled it—along with my bra, over my head and tossed them both to the floor. He looked down at me, his eyes slowly roaming over every inch of my body, and the heat of his stare caused goosebumps to prickle against my skin. A warmth washed over me when he whispered, "So fucking beautiful."

His phone started to ring, but he ignored it as he lowered his mouth to my shoulder. He trailed kisses past my collarbone down to my breasts, and heavy breaths and low moans filled the room as he took my nipple into his mouth. While he continued to nip and suck along the curves of my breast, he moved inside of me with slow, shallow thrusts. My God, he felt so good. His mouth. His hands. His cock. I was already in complete sensory overload when he started to increase his pace. His movements suddenly became rough and demanding as he took me deeper and harder.

"Yes!" I cried as I tightened around him. I was getting close, and when Shadow's body grew taut, there was no doubt that he was as well. We were completely in sync as he slid his hands underneath my backside to lift me higher, and as he angled his position, he instantly found the spot he knew would send us both over the edge. Seconds later, my orgasm ripped through me, and I heard him let out a gratified groan, as he thrust into me one last time, giving in to his own release.

After several moments, he slowly eased off me and moved down on the sofa next to me, pulling me over to him. I let my head fall back on his chest as I listened to the sounds of our erratic breathing slow into a steady rhythm. His phone chimed for the second time, and I felt his muscles tense beneath me. The longer he sat there holding me, the more anxious he became. Something about that missed message was obviously worrying him, so I asked, "Do you need to get that?"

"Yeah, I do," he grumbled. I watched as he reached into

his jeans and pulled it out of his back pocket. When he looked down at the screen, an aggravated expression crossed his face. "Damn."

"What? Is something wrong?"

He quickly stood and tossed his condom in the trash before pulling up his jeans. "I'm sorry, but something's come up and I've gotta go."

"Okay," I muttered as I watched him buckle his belt.

Sensing something was wrong, he asked, "You okay?"

I couldn't tell him the truth without sounding completely pathetic, so I lied. "Yes, I'm good."

"*Alex*."

"I guess I'm just a little disappointed that you're leaving so soon."

He leaned down and placed his hands on the back of the sofa as he hovered over me. "Just to be clear, I wouldn't be leaving now if I had a choice in the matter. My brothers need me, and I've gotta go."

"Okay. I understand." When he cocked his eyebrow, I smiled and said, "Really, I do."

He kissed me once more, then stood up and said, "I tried to warn you about me."

"You did?" I teased.

"I did. You should've listened."

"Maybe so, but I'll take my chances."

SHADOW

Even after a twenty-minute bike ride back to the clubhouse, I could still smell her on my skin, making it impossible not to remember how good she felt in my arms. I never dreamed anyone could get to me the way she did. I'd been void of feeling for so long, I didn't know I was even capable of letting someone in. I'd spent years guarding myself from all the pain and heartache that came from getting too close, but without even trying, this woman had torn down my walls and shown me a world I'd forgotten even existed. They were feelings I thought I didn't need—thought I didn't deserve—but now that I'd gotten a taste of just how incredibly good it could be, I only wanted more. As much as I hated to admit it, Alex had become an addiction, and I was already jonesing for another hit. I'd still be at her place satisfying that craving if I hadn't gotten the call from Blaze telling me that two more of our dealers had been found dead.

By the time I made it inside the clubhouse, all the guys were already gathered for church. I made my way over to my place at the table, and once everyone else was settled, Gus called us to attention. "B.W. and Michaels were taken out tonight. Killed in their own fucking homes before they even had a chance to get on the streets. I'm done with this shit. I want to know who the fuck is responsible, and I want their fucking head on a goddamn platter."

Riggs turned to him and said, "I was about to track down Jasper's cousin, Milton. Got his address and linked into his phone."

"Good. I want eyes on him tonight." He paused before continuing, "I don't want prospects on this. It's too fucking important. Blaze and Murphy take the first shift, then you and Shadow can take over in the morning."

"Understood. Once we have Jasper, maybe we can get it out of him who he's working with."

"Oh, we'll get it out of him. I'll make damn well sure of it," I assured him.

Moose leaned forward and added, "I have no doubt that you will, but in the meantime, we gotta do something more to protect our guys. The rotations clearly aren't enough. These motherfuckers are going into their homes ... with their wives and children. That's fucking bullshit. We need to bring them in for a lockdown before anyone else ends up getting hurt."

"Agreed. We'll have them all come in, and they don't go anywhere without one of the brothers by their side."

Moose nodded. "I'll make the call and have them all here by morning."

Gus's face grew grim as he said, "As you all know, we're still trying to get a handle on everything that went down with the Culebras. Riggs has been busting his ass to find intel on them, but even with everything he's been able to uncover, there's still so much we just don't know yet."

"You think they may be behind this?" Blaze interrupted.

"Got no idea. The fact is, we cost those motherfuckers millions when we took out that warehouse. I don't know when or where, but there's going to be blowback from that. Keeping that in mind, I hate to think we have another war approaching, but with what's been going down, I've got no doubt that we do."

Murphy clenched his fist as he barked, "Then, we do what we've always done. We find these motherfuckers and shut them down."

"That's exactly what we're gonna do, but until we find these assholes, we've gotta be prepared. Keep your eyes and ears open, and never let your guard down for any reason."

Gus dismissed church, and using the information that Riggs had provided, he sent Murphy and Blaze to start their surveillance of Milton. While I was completely invested in bringing down the men who were threatening the club, that didn't mean I'd forgotten about my concerns over Alex's apartment. Her security was subpar at best, and it was only a matter of time before it became an issue. Knowing I couldn't live with that, I followed Riggs out into the hall. As the club's computer hacker and security guru, I hoped that he'd be able to help. He was caught by surprise when I said, "Hey, brother, I need a favor."

"Really? What kind of favor?"

"I got a place that needs an upgrade on security."

"Okay. What kind of upgrade are we talking about? Cameras? Locks? Lights?"

"Yes."

He chuckled. "Gonna need more than that, Shadow."

"It needs the works. I need to know she's safe."

Sounding fairly shocked, he asked, "*She*? Who are we talking about?"

"*A* friend, Riggs."

"Is this a *special* friend?" He smirked. "I need to know what I'm working with here."

"Can you update the security or not?"

"Yeah. I can do that. Just need the address. I'll get the guys to install it first thing in the morning. Will that suffice?"

"Morning will be fine. Her name is Alex. I'll text you the address."

When I turned to leave, he teased. "I'll take care of your girl for ya, brother, but that shit's gonna cost ya!"

"Never doubted that for a second," I grumbled as I headed back to my room. After a long, hot shower, I lay down on my bed, and it wasn't long before my mind started to drift back to Alex. A warm feeling crept over me as I thought about the soothing sound of her voice, the soft caress of her lips, and the incredible feeling of her hands on my body. She had me completely captivated, and as I closed my eyes, I wanted to remember every detail of our night together, hoping the memories would be enough to keep the nightmares at bay. Unfortunately, that didn't happen. As I finally started to doze off, that familiar uneasiness started to weigh down on me. I knew the dreams were coming. I had no idea where they planned to take me, but I knew it wouldn't be a pleasant memory. None of them ever were. Between my childhood and my time in Afghanistan, I had no good memories. I tried to fight my latest nightmare, but my exhaustion won out and in a matter of seconds, I was drifting into the past.

I was standing on the front porch of my fourth and final home with Ms. Haliburton by my side. It was a quaint, two-story brick home, and while it looked like a decent place, there was something about it that gave me an unsettled feeling, but then all the foster homes did. I was eleven years old when my family was taken from me. There was no one to take me in, no family or friends waiting with open arms to love me like their own, so I was placed in foster care and forced to live with complete strangers. I thought losing my parents and sister, the people who I loved most in the world, was the worst thing that could possibly happen to me, but I was wrong—very, very wrong. After Ms. Haliburton knocked on the door, she looked over to me with a reassuring smile. She had good intentions, but it didn't help the anxiety growing in the pit of my stomach. We'd only been waiting a few seconds when the door eased open, revealing an attractive blonde wearing a plaid button-down and a pair of dark denim jeans. A smile spread across her face as she said, "Well, hello there. You must be Mason. I'm Janice Ridley. It's so good to finally meet you. Mrs. Haliburton has told me so much about you."

Just as the words had come out of her mouth, a man stepped up behind Mrs. Ridley. His salt and pepper hair was brushed perfectly to the side, and he wore a navy suit. He forced a smile and said, "Mrs. Haliburton. Nice see you again."

"Hello, Cal. I know I'm a little early, but I was eager for you to meet Mason."

"And we are eager to meet him as well." He looked down at me and smiled. "Hi, Mason. I'm Cal Ridley."

It took me a moment to respond, but I finally managed to mumble, "Hello, Mrs. Ridley. Mr. Ridley."

She motioned us both inside. "Come on in, and I'll introduce you to the rest of the crew."

Mrs. Haliburton placed her hand on my back, nudging me forward, and my heart started to race as I walked inside the house. I took a quick glance around and was relieved to see that the inside was just as nice as the outside. It was far from fancy, but it was much better than the shabby apartment I was staying in just a few nights before. As we stepped into the living room, we were greeted by the Ridleys' other foster children. They were all sitting on the sofa, each of them silently staring at me as we approached. Mr. Ridley stood by his wife as she said, "Kids, this is Mason ... the young man I've been telling you about."

I lifted my hand in a slight wave and said, "Hey."

"Let me introduce you to everyone." She walked over to a young boy who was about seven or so with blond hair, blue eyes, and a smile that was filled with innocence. "This is Grady. You'll be sharing a room with him, but don't worry, there's plenty of space for you both."

I nodded and replied, "Nice to meet you, Grady."

"The twins are Brooklyn and Brea. It might take you a little while to tell them apart, but I'm sure you'll figure it out." She was right. The two brown-headed girls were dressed in the same blue-striped shirt and denim shorts with their hair pulled back using the same colored ribbon. Their facial features were nearly identical, but I noticed one of the girls had freckles on the bridge of her nose. My focus was still on the twins when Mrs. Ridley turned to the oldest of the children and said, "And finally, we have Michele."

At thirteen years old, Michele was the oldest of all the children in the house, and she was quite beautiful with long dark-

brown hair and crystal blue eyes. She gave me a half-smile as she straightened her back and said, "Hi, Mason."

There was something odd about the way she looked at me that made me think she was trying to warn me of something, but I had no idea what it could be. Shaking it off as my imagination, I replied, "Hi, Michele."

We spent the next half hour trying to muddle through all the small talk, and once Mrs. Haliburton felt like I was ready, she slipped out, leaving me alone with the Ridleys. It didn't take me long to figure out that there was something very different about my new family. Even though there were five children in their home, the house was eerily quiet. The kids stayed locked away in their rooms, spending their entire day in complete and utter silence. With each moment that passed, I became more and more curious about their odd behavior. Hoping for answers, I walked over to Michele's room to ask her what was going on. She was sitting at her desk, working on her homework, and didn't even look up when I walked into the room. "You can't be in here, Mason. Go back to your room."

"But—"

She turned and with an intense expression, she warned, "No buts. It's getting late. You need to be in bed. Besides, if they find you in here, we're both gonna get it. Now, do what I said and go back to your room."

"Gonna get it? What are you talking about?" I pushed.

"I hate to break it to you, kid, but you didn't just move in with the Brady Bunch."

Just as the words came out of her mouth, her blue eyes widened with fear as she listened to the sounds of his footsteps creeping down the hall. "What's wrong?"

"He's coming," Michele whispered to me with warning in her voice. "You've gotta get out of here. Now!"

I was just about to turn to leave when Cal appeared in the doorway. As soon as he saw me, his face twisted into an angry scowl and I could smell the alcohol on his breath as he barked, "What the hell are you doing in here?"

"He was just asking me about school," Michele lied.

"You really expect me to believe that?" he growled. "I know why he's in here. He's hoping to get himself a piece, and that shit isn't gonna happen!"

He reared back and slammed the back of his hand across my cheek. When I stumbled back, he reached for my throat, squeezing tightly as he slammed me against the wall. "Cal, don't! He didn't know any better!"

"Well, he's about to learn how things work around here!" He pounded his fist into my side, nearly breaking several of my ribs, and I fell to the floor. His foot came crashing into my side as he shouted, "You'll do as you're told, boy, or you'll pay the fucking consequences."

After several more firm kicks, he reached down and grabbed a fist full of my hair, dragging me over to Michele's closet. He opened the door and tossed me inside. He slammed the door, and I was left cowering on the floor like a wounded animal. I was completely stunned. My parents rarely ever spanked me, and they certainly never hit me like my new foster father had just done. I didn't know what to think, and as I sat there wiping the tears from my eyes and the blood from my mouth, I heard the sounds of whimpering coming through the door. It was clear that he was hurting her and even though I was desperate to help her, I could only sit there and listen. Eventually, the room grew quiet, and I heard him stumble out of the room. I sat there for hours waiting for someone to let me out of the closet, but it wasn't until the following morning when Mrs. Ridley finally came.

The door flew open and she towered over me with a cold, angry scowl as she snarled, "Get up! You're late!"

The dream ended there. I wasn't forced to remember the events that followed, but those memories clung to me like a wet blanket as I lay there staring at the ceiling. Eventually, I rolled over and managed to go back to sleep, if you could call it that, but after a couple of hours tossing and turning, I woke up to the sun blaring through the window. I lay there for another half hour then pulled myself out of bed and got dressed. I was eager to see if there had been any word from Murphy and Blaze, so I went to find Riggs. When he wasn't in his room, I headed to the kitchen and found Cyrus, T-Bone, and Gunner sitting at the table eating breakfast. I made a cup of coffee then sat down next to Gunner. He looked up at me and asked, "How's it going, brother?"

"It's going. You seen Riggs?"

After months of healing from an almost fatal gunshot wound, it was good to see that he was finally getting back to his old self, even if that meant he was back to running his mouth. Gunner's mouth twisted into a mischievous smirk as he announced, "Yeah. He left about a half hour ago with a couple of prospects. Said he was going to install a security system for a *friend* of yours."

"Riggs talks too fucking much," I growled, stopping him midsentence.

Just as he was about to respond, Jasmine, one of the club girls, came over and asked, "Hey, Shadow. You want me to fix you a plate?"

"No, I'm good," I grumbled.

She spun around and headed back to the stove as Cyrus turned to me and said, "Riggs said your friend owns the bookstore on Broad Street. She any relation to Hallie?"

While I knew there was more behind the story, I repeated what Alex had told me. "Hallie was her grandmother."

"Hmm ... Don't guess I ever knew she had a granddaughter, but I remember a few years back when this girl—"

Before he could finish his sentence, our burners all chimed at once. We reached into our pockets to pull them out, and I looked down at the screen and saw that the message was from Gus. Blaze and Murphy had tracked down Jasper at his warehouse, but there was a hitch—he wasn't there alone. There were armed guards surrounding the building, and it was up to us to help them get Jasper out of there. As soon as we finished reading our orders, T-Bone stood up and said, "Looks like it's party time, boys."

We all stood up and rushed towards the parking lot. When we got outside, Moose, Vet, and Mack were already on their bikes. T-Bone went over and joined them, and once Gunner and I got in his SUV, the guys followed us towards Jasper's warehouse. While we were all ready to get our hands on Jasper, I was feeling especially eager. I knew it was just a matter of putting the pieces of the puzzle together, and then we'd finally find out who was fucking with the club. The day of reckoning was near, and I looked forward to executing our revenge.

ALEX

For as long as I could remember, I'd always had this unexplainable feeling that *something* was out there waiting for me that I had been missing in my life—something life altering—but it was just out of my reach. Over the past few weeks that feeling had grown stronger, making me feel restless and on edge. As I lay in bed and thought back over my night with Shadow, I realized that when I was with him, that restlessness just wasn't there; I felt whole and at peace—like I could truly be myself. Yet, as much as I liked that feeling, it terrified me, mainly because it could never last. Shadow had no idea who I really was. He knew nothing about my past and what I'd run away from, and even if I wanted to tell him, I couldn't. The risk was just too high. Besides, it wasn't like he would understand. How could he? There were times when I didn't even understand it myself.

For the past eight years I had been Alex Carpenter, the bookstore owner whose past wasn't lined with deceit and heartbreak, but it was all just a farce. She was just a fictional character I portrayed so I could escape the darkness I'd left behind. It wasn't difficult to play the part. Hell, I'd been pretending my entire life. It was something I'd learned from the person I loved most in the world, my mother. She'd gotten so good at acting that, not only did she have me convinced, she'd convinced herself. Like me, she wanted desperately to believe that the stories she told me about my father were true, but unfortunately, they weren't. In actuality, my father wasn't a typical business man. He worked long hours, attended late night meetings, and flew all over the world; but doing so wasn't simply a means to provide for his family—not even close. The truth was, my father was one of the most infamous drug traders in California, and his so-called business was filled with secrets, lies, and illegal activity that he kept hidden from everyone around him, including my mother and me.

I believed the stories my mother told me, mainly because I had no reason not to. I rarely laid eyes on my father. He spent every waking moment locked away in his office or traveling, and we rarely even crossed paths. If I did happen to run into him, it was only for a fleeting moment. There were times when it troubled me how he didn't seem bothered by the fact that he didn't really know me. He had no idea what I liked, my favorite color, or favorite foods. My father was clueless as to who my friends were or that I was an honor student. Mom would try to assure me that he loved me, but it was just a lie. The truth was: My father was a monster who was driven by his thirst for power and money, and when it came to me, I was simply one of his many possessions—nothing more than one of his portraits that hung on the wall. The revelation that my father was nothing more than a low-life criminal was difficult to accept, but it was even harder when I discovered just how cold-hearted and malicious he could truly be.

I hated him with every fiber of my being for what he'd done. I left home and never once considered going back. As much as I wanted to forget my father and the heartache he'd caused, I lived in constant fear that one day he'd come looking for me and find a way to force me back into his world. The thought of that alone made me realize I would always be looking over my shoulder. I could never truly be free, and falling in love just wasn't an option. As much as I wanted to let my guard down with Shadow, I couldn't, not even for a second, for I feared that once I let him in, I'd only end up hurting us both. The thought of it saddened me.

While I was wallowing in my self-pity, I heard odd noises coming from just outside my building. I lay there listening to the different banging sounds until I eventually rolled over to check the time. It was a little after six in the morning, which was way too early for my neighbors to be up. Overcome with curiosity, I got out of bed and threw on some clothes. Once I was downstairs, I looked out the window and was shocked to see a man standing on a ladder while two men stood on the ground next to him, handing him equipment as they talked back and forth. I hadn't been notified of any maintenance work, and certainly didn't order it myself, so I had no idea what they were doing. I leaned forward for a better look and noticed they were all wearing a Satan's Fury cut.

Confused and wondering what they were up to, I quickly unlocked the door and stuck my head outside, then asked the guy up on the ladder, "Who are you, and what exactly are you doing up there?"

"Hey there, doll. The name's Riggs." His lips curled into a smile, and his brown eyes sparkled with mischief as they skirted over me. "You must be Alex."

Riggs was one of those tall, dark, and handsome types, and while there was no doubt that plenty of women would find him attractive, I was too preoccupied to care *what* he looked like. "Okay, *Riggs*. You want to tell me what you are doing up there?"

"What? You mean Shadow didn't tell ya?"

A curious look crossed his face as I answered, "Umm … no. I guessed it slipped his mind last night. He mentioned that something important was going on with his brothers, and the next thing I knew he was gone. I haven't heard anything from him since."

"Yeah, well … things like that happen from time to time." I didn't miss how he hadn't confirmed or denied Shadow's allegations that something *was going on,* and even though I was tempted to push the subject, he didn't give me a chance. He motioned his hands up towards the camera he was mounting to the side of my building and said, "We're installing a new security system for you. Lights. Cameras. Locks. The works."

"And *why* are you doing that?"

"Cause Shadow asked me to," he answered in a matter-of-fact tone.

"Any idea why Shadow would ask you to do that without telling me?" I grumbled.

"'Cause he's Shadow," he snickered.

"I don't even know what that's supposed to mean, but

that's beside the point. You need to stop, 'cause there's no way I can afford all this."

"It's all good. There's no charge."

"What do you mean *no charge*? This has to cost a fortune!"

"Yeah, but that's not for you to worry about."

Becoming aggravated, I snapped, "What do you mean 'it's not for you to worry about'? Who do you think is paying for all this?"

Just then, his phone started ringing, and he pulled it out of his pocket and answered, "Yeah?"

After a three-second conversation, he climbed down from his ladder and rushed towards his truck then said, "I've gotta jet, but my guys will get this finished up."

"Wait." I started to follow him as I shouted, "You haven't answered my question!"

"You're asking the wrong man, doll." He turned and gave a few orders to his biker buddies then climbed inside his truck. He started to pull away from the curb but stuck his head out the window to inform me, "Once they get done installing everything out here, they're gonna need access to the inside."

Before I could refuse, he'd already hit the gas and disappeared into the flow of traffic. I let out a deep breath and turned to the younger of the two men Riggs had left behind. "Can you at least tell me what you're going to be *installing*?"

"We're putting up two cameras out here and two more in the back of the building so you can monitor all the entrances." He started up the ladder as he continued, "Then, we're gonna add a couple of security lights and new locks on all the doors, including upstairs in your apartment."

"My apartment?"

"Yes, ma'am. We'll mount a camera and security lights up there, too."

"Is all that really necessary?"

"You never know." The sun was starting to bear down on us, and sweat trickled across his brow as he shrugged. "Better to be safe than sorry and all that."

"But ... I didn't ask Shadow to do all this."

"He's just trying to make sure nothing happens to you, and I can't say I blame him." He looked down at me with his eyebrow cocked high. "If I was Shadow and had a hot girl like you living and working in an area like this, I'd be doing the same damn thing."

Before I had a chance to comprehend what he'd just said, his buddy handed him a long cable of wires and said, "Hey, man, if we wanna get this shit done before the store opens, we better get rolling."

"Yeah, Skeeter, I know. I'm working on it," he complained.

"I guess I'll let you get to it," I told them as I started towards the door. "But I expect you to leave me a bill when you're done. There's no way I'm letting Shadow pay for all of this."

He nodded. "I'll see what I can do. By the way, my name's Turnpike. If you need something, just let me know."

"Thanks, Turnpike. I will." As I turned back towards my door, a thought crossed my mind. Even though it was early, the temperature was already scorching hot and the humidity was climbing by the second. I glanced back over to the two bikers and couldn't help but wonder why they hadn't chosen something more comfortable to wear. Curious, I asked, "Hey, Turnpike. Can I ask you something?"

"Sure."

"This may sound like a crazy question, but why are you wearing those hot leather vests? It's like ninety-five degrees out here. Aren't you miserable?"

"Honestly, they aren't as hot as you might think, but even if they were, I wouldn't go anywhere without my cut," he answered proudly. "Besides, wearing them today helps you just as much as it does us."

More confused than ever, I mumbled, "Huh?"

"People see members of Satan's Fury out here working on your store, they're gonna think twice before fucking with you," he explained. "And they sure as hell aren't gonna get in our way while we're working. Simple as that."

"Oh."

"I'll let you know when we need to get inside."

"Okay," I answered as I started upstairs.

I contemplated everything he'd said as I headed to the bathroom and started my shower. I'd never really thought of myself as a judgmental person, but there was something about his answer that stuck out in my mind. When he mentioned people seeing Satan's Fury working on my store, it made me wonder if that was actually a good thing. Like most folks who lived in the city, I'd heard the stories about Satan's Fury, and while I had no idea if all of it was true, it had made an impression on me—a not-so-good impression. I had no doubt that the same was true for lots of people in the area, and I had to consider the ramifications of my store being associated with the club. Everything I had was wrapped up in the success of my little business, and if it went south, I'd have nothing. That image terrified me, but at the same time, something told me it wasn't necessarily all that bad either, especially when I thought about all the money I'd lost from thugs who'd stolen from me. Theft and vandalism were big problems in my neighborhood. As much as I hated the thought of losing the little bit of Hallie that still lingered in the bookstore, I'd often considered moving to a new location. Starting over would take money, *lots of money*, and it simply wasn't an option. So, I figured my best bet was to just pay for the new security system and pray that my loyal customers wouldn't be steered away by the presence of Shadow's brothers.

Once I was dressed, I went downstairs to let Turnpike and Skeeter inside so they could finish installing the new locks. After they were done, they headed upstairs to work on whatever they needed to do up there. While they were busy, I set about getting everything ready to open the store. I'd just finished making the coffee when Turnpike came in. He walked over and handed me a new set of keys and said, "We've got everything up and running."

"Okay. Thanks. I really appreciate it."

"No problem."

"Can you do me a favor?" I asked as I headed over to the counter.

"Sure. Whatever you need."

After I filled out a check, I handed to him and said, "Can you give this to Shadow? It's all I can afford right now, but I'll get him the rest as soon as I can."

His face twisted into a grimace as he glanced down at

the check. "I don't know. Maybe you should talk to him about this first."

"There's nothing to talk about. I'm going to pay for everything. It's just going to take a little time," I answered firmly.

"Okay, but he's not gonna like it."

"Maybe not, but that's the way it's going to be. Anyway, I really do appreciate you and Skeeter doing all this today."

"It's been a pleasure." As he started for the door, he shouted, "Hope to see ya around!"

"You too!"

Once they were both gone, I strolled over to the front door and turned the *Open* sign around then glanced out the window. I wasn't surprised to see that Shadow was nowhere in sight. Even though he had my number, he hadn't used it, and I hated that it bothered me so much, especially since I'd spent my entire morning going over all the reasons why getting involved with Shadow was a bad idea. While mine were totally justifiable, it irked me to think he might've had the same doubts I'd been having. Maybe it was all just in my head. Maybe he was *just busy*, but even so, he could've touched base to at least warn me that his brothers were coming by. *Something*. The whole thing was getting under my skin, and seeing how he hadn't shown up for his morning coffee just added salt to the wound. Thankfully it was Saturday, the busiest day of the week, and without Debbie here to help me with the customers, I didn't have time to dwell on it.

Things started to slow down as lunchtime rolled around, and I was able to finally catch my breath.

I was just about to grab myself a cup of coffee and a

bite to eat when I heard the front door open. At first, I thought it was just another customer coming in to browse, but a peculiar sensation suddenly washed over me, making the hairs on the back of my neck stand tall. Without even looking, I knew it wasn't just some random customer. Instead, it was someone from my past, someone I'd hoped that I'd never have to see again. With my heart pounding against my chest, I slowly turned around, and my worst fears were confirmed when I saw him standing there. Other than a few defined wrinkles and gray hairs, he looked exactly the same. The same body. The same intense, dark eyes. Even his voice sounded the same as he said, "Hello, Alejandra. It's been a while."

"Yes, it has. I wish I could say that it's good to see you," I spat. "What are you doing here, *Marcus*?"

SHADOW

There are two ways to initiate an attack: sneak in quietly, and do your best not to be seen as you take out the enemy one by one, or bust in—full throttle with guns a blazing and wipe out your adversaries in a matter of seconds. Considering the fact that Gus's patience had worn thin, it came as no surprise he chose the latter. We'd lost four of our men in a week and had no idea who was truly behind the attacks. The man with all the answers was just within our reach, and we were all ready to find out exactly what he knew. Gus motioned for us to move forward as soon as we got off our bikes, and like a pack of hungry wolves, we advanced towards the warehouse, keeping our focus on all the windows and doors. Like most of the buildings in the area, it was old and dilapidated with local gang tags spray-painted all over the metal exterior, and most of the windows were already destroyed, making it easier to see inside. There was trash and debris strewn from the front to the back of the building, making it clear that Jasper had no pride in his business.

As soon as the front guard noticed us charging towards him, he lifted his weapon and pointed it in our direction. Unfortunately for him, Gus already had his Glock drawn, and before the guard even had a chance to fire, Gus pulled his trigger and killed him on the spot. By the time his lifeless body fell to the ground, four more guards made their appearance. Gus turned to T-Bone and Murphy and ordered, “Cover the back. Don’t want that motherfucker slipping through our fingers.”

With a quick nod, the pack divided, and in a matter of seconds we’d surrounded the entire building. Thankfully, we were on the outskirts of town, so we didn’t have to worry about being heard as the explosion of gunfire erupted around us. With each guard who was taken down, we continued to move forward until we were just a few yards away from the front door. Once he felt the coast was clear, Gus pointed to the door, giving the go ahead for me and Murphy to enter. As we stepped forward, Murphy turned to me and said, “I’ll go in first. Cover me.”

I followed him through the door, and we’d only taken a couple of steps when gunshots were fired from the left side of the room. As soon as I spotted the shooter, I aimed my gun at his head and squeezed the trigger, taking him out before he had a chance to fire off another shot. We surveyed the area closely with each new step while slowly continuing forward, and it wasn’t long before I noticed Gus, Riggs, and T-Bone slipping through one of the side doors. They fired off several additional shots behind us, and after they took out the last of the guards, T-Bone shouted, “Clear!”

With a quick nod, Murphy started towards the office door. He extended his hand, and just as he was reaching for the doorknob, a round of bullets blasted through the wooden door. As he lunged to his right, Murphy growled, "Goddammit!"

I shot off several rounds directly in the center of the door, and after I heard a loud thud against the floor, the gunshots stopped. With my Glock aimed straight ahead, I lifted my foot and slammed it into the door, and as it burst open, Jasper darted out of my line of sight. He slipped behind his bodyguard—a massive African-American male who was at least six foot seven with muscles bulging from head to toe, including a neck that was as thick as a tree stump. The guy was intimidating to say the least, and the fact that he had an AR pointed at my chest didn't help matters. I inhaled a deep breath and tried to think about my next move when Murphy and the others came up behind me. The man's eyes grew fierce, and like an animal that had been backed into a corner, it was clear that he was prepared to do whatever it took to fight his way out.

I kept the barrel of my gun trained at his head and said, "*Drop it.*"

"And why would I do that?" he asked as his finger twitched against the trigger. I wasn't sure which surprised me more, his high-pitched, feminine voice or the fact that his fingernails were painted a bright shade of pink. It was then that I realized he wasn't Jasper's bodyguard after all.

"Because it's the only way you're gonna get out of here alive, Milton."

He cocked his eyebrow as he spat, "We both know I'm

not getting out of here alive, but at least I can take you with me when I go."

"We're not here for you," Gus told him as he stepped up beside me. "We just want Jasper. Hand him over, and we'll be on our way."

"What do you want with him anyway?"

"That's between him and me," Gus growled.

"What is it about you Satan's Fury boys? It's like you think you own the whole goddamn city."

"That's because we do, and if you know what's good for you, you'll hand over Jasper and be on your way." Gus took a step towards him. "Cause if you don't ... and you even think about pulling that fucking trigger, I'll do things to you that you can't begin to imagine. Hell, you'll be begging me to put a fucking bullet in your head, and once I'm done with you, I'll go after every fucking person you've ever cared about or even *thought of* caring about, and I'll do the same fucking thing to them. You got me?"

"Don't listen to him." Jasper's beady, little eyes filled with panic as he pleaded, "If you hand me over to them, there's no telling what they'll do to me."

Lowering his rifle, Milton turned and looked at Jasper as he said, "I tried to warn you, but you were just too damn stubborn to listen. Now, you're gonna have to face this thing head on."

"But it wasn't me." Jasper's back stiffened as he continued, "I wasn't the one who took out their guys."

"Stop with the bullshit, Jasper. No one wants to hear your fucking lies, especially me," Gus growled as he took the rifle out of Milton's hand. "I know you're in cahoots with someone, and one way or another, I'm gonna find out exactly who it is. So do us both a favor and save us some time and trouble. Tell me what I want to know."

"I already told you. I didn't have anything to do with it."

"Alright then. Have it your way." Gus looked over to me and said, "Take them back to the clubhouse."

"Wait! What?" Milton shrieked. "You said you'd let me go."

I shook my head. "I said you'd walk out of here alive, and you are."

"That's bullshit, man. I didn't have anything to do with this shit!"

"We'll see about that," Gus grumbled. "Get them out of here."

As Murphy and I started to lead them out of the office, Riggs asked Gus, "What do you want us to do about cleaning up this mess?"

"You and Blaze gather up anything we might need out of here … computers, files, whatever—and load it in the truck." He looked over to T-Bone and instructed, "You and Cyrus help the prospects clean the area. Make sure you clear our tracks, then light a match to the place."

"You got it."

Murphy and I zip-tied Milton and Jasper's hands behind their backs, then took them out to the SUV. They both reminded me of an old married couple when Milton glared at Jasper and whined, "I'll never forgive you for this."

With a roll of his eyes, Jasper mumbled, "You weren't complaining when I bought you that fucking BMW last week."

"That's because I didn't know it was blood money that bought it."

"Blood money, huh?" I growled as I grabbed Milton and shoved him in the back of the SUV. Glaring at him with all the sarcasm I could muster, I added, "Gotta wonder how you knew about that." And then I slammed the door.

After that, Milton didn't say another word. Once we had them both secured in the vehicle, we drove straight to the clubhouse and led them both inside. While Murphy put Milton in a room, I took Jasper on a little tour of the building, starting with Boon's holding room. When I eased the door open and the foul odor of the room started billowing out, Jasper winced with repulsion. It was clear from his expression that he wasn't prepared to see his employee bound to a wall with blood and bruises covering his entire body. In his weakened state, Boon was barely able to lift his head, but when he noticed Jasper standing there, utter defeat flashed through his swollen eyes. "Fuck, boss. I was hoping you were gonna find a way to get me outta here."

"I might've been able to help you if you hadn't run your goddamn mouth, dumbass. I should've known I couldn't trust you."

"You don't understand. I took all I could take, boss. I really did," Boon complained.

Remembering how hard he'd fought to keep his boss's secret, I turned to Boon and asked, "You reckon he could do any better?"

"Got no idea."

Jasper's entire body stiffened when I replied, "Well, don't worry. I'm about to find out."

Without giving either of them a chance to respond, I closed the door. Sensing that things were about to take a turn for the worse, Jasper started to resist, but he didn't get very far as I tugged him down to the next room. I opened the door, revealing Hoss bound to his chair exactly the way I'd left him. Jasper's eyes widened with horror as he gasped, "What the fuck did you do to him?"

Ignoring Jasper's comment, Hoss turned his attention to me as he pleaded, "See. I told you how to find him. I done what you asked. Now, will you let me out of this fucking chair? It's killing me, man. I can't take it any longer."

"What the hell is this place?" Jasper asked.

I closed the door and shoved Jasper further down the hall. All of the holding rooms were taken which left only one empty room in the hall. While I'd never used it during an interrogation, I decided it was the perfect place for Jasper. I opened the door and pushed him inside my storage room. As soon as he caught sight of all my tools and devices, he started to cry and thrash about from side to side as he shouted, "Oh, God! What the fuck are you going to do to me?"

The man had lost all self-control, and I had no problem bringing him back to reality. I knocked him out with a swift uppercut to the jaw, causing him to flail backwards onto the floor and fall like a toppled tree. While he was out, I removed his zip ties and replaced them with metal cuffs, then lifted him off the ground. Once I'd secured his cuffs to a hook in the ceiling, I released him, leaving him swinging from his restraints. After several seconds, he finally started to come around. When his eyes started to flutter open, I said, "Welcome back."

His voice was shaking as he muttered, "Man, you gotta listen to me. This is all just a big misunderstanding. You've got the wrong guy."

"Um-hmm."

"No! Seriously. You've gotta listen to me! I didn't do anything. I've been careful. I've followed the rules. I've kept my distance and stayed out of your territory. I've done right by Satan's Fury. I swear it."

As I reached for a pair of gardening sheers, I told him, "I should warn you, Jasper. I don't have much patience for liars."

"But I ain't—"Jasper stopped midsentence as soon as I took a step towards him. His face contorted into a painful grimace when I placed the sheers at the tip of his finger, snipping off the first inch or so. It was a subtle but extremely painful technique that I'd use to subdue my target, and as soon as the pain started to register in his brain, he bellowed, "Oh, fuck me! You cut off my fucking finger!"

Ignoring him, I placed the sheers further down on his finger, applying pressure as I growled, "I need you to listen to me, Jasper."

"Please!"

"Jasper, are you listening to me?" I pushed as I pressed down a little firmer, causing his finger to bleed even more.

"Yes! I'm listening!"

"Good." Without releasing the pressure on the sheers, I continued, "Now that I have your attention … I want you to think back to Boon and Hoss. I want you to think about the hell they've been through. And I gotta tell ya—they both went through a lot before they finally started talking, but the fact is … they answered my questions. Hell, they told me exactly what I needed to know and more. *And so will you*. This pain you're feeling right now is nothing. It's just a drop in the hat compared to what you've got coming if you don't give me every bit of intel on this guy."

"You don't understand … He'll kill me if I breathe a word about him."

"Oh, hell. You really are thick in the head," I scoffed. "Don't you get it? You're dead either way, asshole. There's no walking away from this, but you tell me what I want to know and I'll take it easy on ya … A quick shot to the head and it's done." My voice grew cold and unsympathetic as I continued, "But you hold out on me, and I'll butcher you —inch by tiny inch—until you finally start talking. And Jasper … *you will talk*. Don't think for one second that you won't."

A look of defeat crossed his face as he replied, "I'll tell you everything, but knowing who he is won't change anything. This guy is like nothing I've ever seen before. He's got an entire army at his fingertips and the type of money most people only dream about. You don't have the kind of manpower you're gonna need to go up against him. Before it's all said and done, he'll kill every last one of ya, and you'll never see him coming. You might as well face it, *tough guy*, you and your fucking club are done, and there's not a damn thing you can do about it."

ALEX

Just *being* in the same room with Marcus made me feel like I'd stepped back in time, and all those old feelings of hurt, anger, and resentment came rushing back. I was so overcome by those emotions, I couldn't move. I simply stood there—staring at the ghost from my past as I tried to come to terms with the fact that he was actually standing right in front of me. There was a time when I trusted Marcus, and I truly believed he cared about me. He made me feel loved in a way that my father never could, but those days were long gone. For so many years I was lied to, manipulated, and deceived until I finally uncovered the truth about my life and all the people in it. I was devastated by my discovery, but sadly, there was no one for me to turn to—no one I could trust, especially Marcus.

I could hear the emotion in his voice as he said, "It's hard to believe that my Alejandra is all grown up."

My entire body tensed at the sound of my given name. I hadn't heard it in almost eight years, and I didn't want to hear it then, especially from him. He had a way of saying it that made me feel special, but I'd learned that I wasn't special at all—to him or my father. "You didn't answer my question, Marcus. What are you doing here?"

Acting as if it was no big deal that he was here, he stepped towards me and said, "Memphis, Tennessee. An interesting choice. I always thought you would've chosen a place like New York City or—"

"New York is overrated. It just so happens that I like it here."

"I can see that. It clearly suits you." He took a quick glance around as he said, "You were lucky that you landed here when you left home. You got a job. A place to stay. A make-believe grandmother. Yeah … I'd say Hallie was a great help to you."

"She was." He'd obviously done his research on my time away from home. I wasn't surprised. Marcus was a man who had a way of uncovering anyone's darkest secrets, and I had no doubt that he knew all of mine. I tried to hide my shaking hands as I said, "I don't know what I would've done without her."

His eyes narrowed as he growled, "Well, you could've come to me."

"Why would I do that? It's not like I could've trusted you not to tell my father that I was planning to leave." My anger helped me forget about my nervousness, and I was finally able to say all the things I'd always wanted to tell him. "After I found out the truth, there was no way in hell that I was going to let either of you stop me from leaving."

"What truth?"

"I know about my mother."

"Your mother?" he asked, sounding confused.

"Stop pretending like you don't know. I know exactly what you and my father let happen to her. I know *everything*."

"I'm not pretending. I seriously have no idea what you're talking about."

"Oh, please," I scoffed. "This whole act is beneath you, Marcus."

"I have no reason to lie to you. I seriously have no idea what you're talking about, Alejandra."

"Oh, man. You're good, Marcus, I'll give you that … but I'm not buying it. Not anymore. I'm done being lied to, so take it somewhere else."

"I'm not lying to you, Ale. You know how I felt about Camilla."

"Yeah, I thought I did, but I was wrong. She was like me—just part of *the job*."

Concern crossed his face as he stepped closer, and I could hear the sincerity in his voice when he said, "No! That's not true. You both were like family to me. You know that!"

"Then, why would you just let her die like that?"

"What exactly was I supposed to do, Ale? She was killed in a car accident."

I ran my hands over my face as I groaned with aggravation. "She didn't die in that car accident, and you damn well know it! The sad thing is you could've stopped it. You could've convinced Dad to help her, then those men wouldn't have—"

"Wait! Stop!" He narrowed his eyes and asked, "What men? What are you talking about?"

I studied him for a moment, and as I saw the disbelief in his eyes, I realized that I'd been wrong to think Marcus had played a part in my mother's death. My voice trembled when I asked, "You really don't know?"

"No, dear. I have no idea what you're talking about. Who are these men?"

"I don't know who they were. I just know they were holding Momma for some kind of ransom. They wanted Dad to pay for her freedom, and when he refused, they tortured her, raped her, and God knows what else."

"When did you find out about this?"

"It was a few months after her funeral. I'd gone up to Dad's office to ask him something. I was about to open the door when I heard him talking on the phone. You know how he hated to be interrupted, so I just stood there and waited for him to finish the call. That's when I heard him talking about it." I felt tears burn my eyes, but I refused to let them fall as I continued, "He was laughing … bragging to whoever was on the other end of the line about how he refused to pay them the money. He said he'd never pay a dime to those idiots. He wouldn't give them the satisfaction of making them think he could be forced to do anything, even if it was to save her."

"Are you sure he was talking about your mother? It could've been anyone."

"It was her. He called her by name, Marcus."

"Damn. I've always known your father was a cold, heartless man, but I never dreamed he would let something like that happen to Camilla."

"We both know she'd have done anything in this world for him." My heart ached as I thought back to my mother. She was the most beautiful woman I'd ever known, inside and out, and I never once doubted her love for me or my father. I saw it in her face, heard it in her voice, and felt it every time she held me in her arms. I missed her dearly, and I hated my father for taking her away from me. "A man who would let that happen to her is nothing but a monster. I wish he was dead."

He reached into his pocket, and as he pulled out an old photograph, he said, "Well, unfortunately, he's not dead. In fact, he's very much alive, and now, he knows everything about you and your new life here in Memphis."

"What?"

"You had to know he would be looking for you." He placed the picture on the counter and slid it over to me. I gave it a quick glance, and my heart sank when I saw that it was a picture of me at the Backyard Dogs concert. I'd seen that very same one in a magazine article that was published right after the concert, but I didn't think it was anything to worry about. It was just my side profile, and it was dark. Apparently it was enough, and now, I was screwed. "I trained you better than this."

"But how?"

"Facial recognition. All it took was that one simple photograph, and after a few months of connecting the dots, he was able to track you down."

"Is that why you've come to see me? Did he send you?"

He shook his head. "No. Your father has no idea I'm here."

"Then, why did you come?"

"To warn you, Alejandra." He shook his head mournfully. "You know how he can be when he wants something, and right now, he's made it his mission to get his daughter back."

"I don't care what his mission is. I'm never going back

there," I snapped. "He's just going to have to accept that I have a life here, and it doesn't include him."

"You wouldn't have run away, changed your name, and stayed hidden for as long as you have if you truly thought that was possible. It's you who has to accept that things can't go the way you want them to. You have to face the fact that your life here is over, but that doesn't mean you can't still have a life." He reached into his back pocket and took out a large envelope. "Here's everything you'll need to get started."

When I peeked inside, I found a new ID, social security card, passport, and enough money to buy two bookstores. Angered at the thought of leaving, I snapped, "No. I'm done running, Marcus. I have a life here … the store, my friends, my home, and I can't just walk away from that."

"You can, and *you will*. You have no other choice. Think about what he did to your mother. What makes you think it will be different with you?"

"Because he doesn't really care about me."

"That's exactly why you should be worried! Think about it. There was a time when he loved and adored your mother, and look at what happened to her. Just think of what he'll do to you." He cocked his eyebrow and continued, "Your father always gets his way no matter what the cost, and right now, he wants you back home. You and I both know he'll stop at nothing to make that happen. Do you really want to see how far he will go?"

My heart ached as I answered, "No. I don't."

"Then, you have to leave." He glanced down at the envelope and said, "There's an address inside. You'll be safe there."

Realizing the risk he'd taken to help me, I asked, "Why

are you doing all this? You have to know that he'd kill you if he ever found out."

"I'm well aware of what he would do." His eyes skirted to the floor as he continued, "I meant what I said. You are like a daughter to me, and I've always loved you like you were my own. From the first moment I laid eyes on you, I knew you didn't belong in that house with him, then after Camilla died, I prayed that you would find your way out. You deserve so much more. You always have. Now that you've found your way out, I plan to do everything in my power to keep you from going back there."

"And you really think this is my only option? There's nothing else I can do?"

"No, Alejandra. There's not."

Accepting my defeat, I asked, "How much time do I have?"

"Not long. If I had to guess, I would say he'll be here by morning."

"Then, I guess I better get my things together."

As he handed me his card, he said, "Here's my number. If you ever need me, I'm just a phone call away."

"Are you leaving?"

"I have some things to tend to, but I will be close … at least until I know you're out of harm's way."

I reached out and hugged him tightly. "Thank you for coming. I'm sorry that I ever doubted you."

"None of that matters now." He took a step back as he looked down at me with concern in his eyes. "I better get going. Remember to call if you need anything."

"I will."

Seconds later, he was gone, and for a brief moment, I wondered if his visit was just a figment of my imagination. Then, I felt the envelope in my hand, and suddenly, the weight of the world came crashing down on me. I looked around the bookstore and started to cry as I thought about all the wonderful memories it held. The thought of having to leave everything I'd worked for, everything and *everyone* I loved behind, I cried and cried some more. After several hours of trying to accept my new-found fate, I wiped the tears from my face and headed upstairs to pack. Searching around my apartment, I grabbed what I could fit into my duffle bag and a couple of boxes. I was about to take the first load out to my car when I heard a strange noise coming from downstairs, and I felt a sudden rush of panic as I remembered that I hadn't locked the front door. Worried that I might've left a customer unattended, I dropped my boxes and rushed downstairs. When I got to the bookstore, I was surprised to find a man hovering over the front counter as he sifted through some of my papers.

I cleared my throat and asked, "Excuse me. Can I help you with something?"

He quickly turned and looked in my direction, and as soon as I saw his face, I recognized him. I studied him for a moment, taking in his size and what weapons he was carrying, and I was surprised to see that he seemed different than I remembered. When I was a kid, I did my best to steer clear of my father's goons, especially Berny. He was tall and slender with a deep, jagged scar that ran across the left side of his face, and he had long, greasy hair that he always kept braided down his back. I was often intimidated by him in the past, but now, he didn't seem nearly as threatening. As I took a step towards him, Berny gave me a wicked grin.

With a sinister smile, he snickered. "Long time no see, Alejandra."

There was no question as to why he was there. He'd come to take me back to my father, and knowing him the way I did, I knew he would use any means necessary to make me go with him. I thought about everything Marcus had taught me as I quickly surveyed the area, doing my best to prepare myself for what was next, because there was no way I was going anywhere without one hell of a fight. I let out a deep breath as I stared him right in the eye and said, "What are you doing here?"

"Your father wants you to come home. He misses you," he answered sarcastically.

"My father doesn't miss me, and you know it."

"Doesn't really matter if he does or doesn't. I'm here to bring you home and that's what I'm going to do."

"Berny, please don't do this. I can't go back there. Not after everything that has happened," I pleaded. "Just let me walk out that door and you can pretend you never saw me."

"That's not going to happen, Ale. If I go back without you, it's my head and you know it."

"I'm not leaving here with you!" I barked.

"Now, isn't that precious. Little Alejandra wants to act all big and tough."

I cocked my head and gave him a coy smile as I sassed, "What makes you think it's an act?"

SHADOW

I had to admit, when Jasper started talking about his new partner—his money and connections, I got an uneasy feeling in my gut. Not because I didn't think the club could handle it, because there was no doubt that we could.

We'd already proven that we had the kind of grit to withstand almost anything, but from the little bit that Jasper had just revealed, we were about to have one hell of a fight on our hands. Unfortunately for Jasper and his new compadre, Satan's Fury had never been scared off from a fight, and this time would be no different. We'd give them the war they were asking for and more. I clamped my hand around Jasper's neck and dug my fingers into his throat as I growled, "Don't waste your breath on the bullshit, asshole. Give me his name."

"I'll tell you everything you need to know, but I need to talk to Gus first."

Angered that he would even consider asking, I

slammed my fist into his gut, causing him to gasp for air. Once he was able to collect himself, I reached for his head, grabbing a handful of hair as I forced him to look at me. "Maybe you haven't noticed, but you're in no position to make demands."

"No disrespect, but he needs to hear this from me. He needs to know first-hand how to deal with this guy, or this thing is gonna end up coming back on me."

"So, what's it to you? I've already told you … your road ends *here*."

"I know. And I get that, but it's already clear you aren't listening to me. This guy is like nothing you've encountered before, and he'll find a way to haunt me long after I'm six feet under. I can't let that happen."

"And why would I give a fuck about that?"

"Please," he begged. "Just give me some time with him, and I swear I'll make it worth y'alls while. I'll tell him everything he needs to know to get to this guy. I give you my word."

"Your word don't mean shit to me, but what-the-fuck-ever. I'll leave it up to Gus to decide if he wants to come down here and talk to you." I reached in my pocket and grabbed my phone as I said, "But I'll tell you this. If you waste his time, my offer of a quick death is off the table."

"Understood."

I sent Gus a text, giving him the rundown on Jasper's request, and to my surprise, he agreed to hear him out. After I read his message, I put my phone back in my pocket, and as I waited for Gus's arrival, I glanced over at Jasper. It was hard to believe that such a tall, lanky piece of shit would have the balls to even consider going against

Fury, and then it hit me: There had to be one hell of a reason why Jasper would take such a huge fucking risk, and it had to be something big—something other than just a handful of cash. Before I had a chance to ask him, Gus stepped into the room and motioned out into the hallway. With a concerned look in his eye, he asked, "What's going on?"

"He's ready to talk, but he's got it in his head that you need to hear what he has to say."

"I'll hear him out, but I gotta tell ya, brother, we're running out of time here. We've got the run at the end of the week." Running his hand through his salt and pepper hair, he continued, "And if that's not enough, Cotton is expecting this shipment to be the biggest one yet. My gut tells me we need to postpone, but the other chapters aren't gonna like it."

Cotton, the president of the Satan's Fury Washington chapter, was the man who worked hand in hand with Gus to implement our pipeline across the country. His club, along with four other of our fellow chapters, had become an integral part of our club's gun distribution ring, and over the past year, it had become more profitable than any of us could've imagined. There was no way Gus would put that in jeopardy, so I wasn't surprised when he mentioned postponing the next pickup. Knowing he was concerned, I tried to assure him by saying, "I learned a long time ago not to question your instincts, Prez. I'm sure Cotton and the others have done the same."

"Let's hope you're right." As he started inside the room, he turned to me and said, "Riggs was asking for you. I think he's got something you need to see."

"You sure you don't want me to stick around?"

"I've got this. I'll let you all know what I find out, and tell Riggs not to go far. Depending on what Jasper says, we may need him."

"You got it."

Once the door closed behind him, I headed out to find Riggs. Thankfully, I didn't have to go far. When I got to his room, he was sitting at his desk, staring at his laptop screen. He didn't budge when I strolled over to him. "Gus said you have something to show me."

"Yeah, but I don't think you're gonna like it."

"What the fuck are you talking about?"

Noting my obvious frustration, Riggs motioned his hand towards his computer screen. It took me a second to realize that it was the video feed from the bookstore, but from what I could tell, the place seemed empty. "A couple of hours ago, your friend had a visitor."

"What kind of a visitor?"

"A guy I've never seen around here before, but it was clear she knew him."

"And?"

"Something about their conversation must've freaked her out, because as soon as he left, she closed the store early and headed upstairs." He paused for a moment, then continued, "I've sent a link to her security feed to your messages. You can use it to monitor what's going on from there."

"Thanks, brother."

"Oh, and I was supposed to give you this." He took a slip of paper from his desk and offered it to me. "Alex wanted you to have it."

I opened the paper and quickly noticed that it was a check from Alex for three hundred dollars. "What's this for?"

"She wanted to pay for the install we did. The boys told her it wasn't necessary, but she demanded that you have it. I figured you would want to handle that."

"Yeah, I'll take care of it," I told him as I ripped up the check.

"Figured you would." He gave me a concerned look as he asked, "Making any leeway with Jasper?"

"He's talking with Gus now. I've got a feeling we're not gonna like what he has to say."

"Yeah, I've got the same fucking feeling, brother, but we'll find our way through it."

"No doubt." As I started for the door, I said, "Thanks again for the help."

"Anytime." I'd only taken a few steps when Riggs shouted, "Hey, Shadow. Hold up!"

I stepped back in the room and asked, "Yeah?"

"Something's up with your girl." He pointed to the screen, and I spotted Alex rushing down her stairs with a large duffle bag strapped across her shoulder. Before I had a chance to register what was going on, the screen flipped to the bookstore, and my blood ran cold when I noticed a strange man standing at her front desk. "You ever see him before?"

I leaned closer to get a better look. "Never."

"Seems strange to get another visit like this so soon. You think something's up with her?"

"No fucking idea, but I'm about to find out."

"You want me to go with you?"

"Not an option, brother. Gus needs you here."

We both watched as Alex made her way into the store, and it was clear from her stunned expression that she wasn't expecting her guest. "Looks like you need to get over there."

"Yeah, let me see what's going on, and then I'll be back."

His eyes narrowed as he said, "Maybe it's nothing, but you don't need to go alone. You've got no idea what you're walking into over there."

"I can handle it." I started towards the door and grabbed my phone to quickly search for the link that Riggs had sent, and once I could see her clearly on the screen, I headed out to my bike. By the time I made it out to the parking lot, I could tell she was in trouble. Relieved to see that Gunner was out by his truck, I yelled "Give me the keys and get in" without giving him an explanation.

After tossing me his keys, he asked, "What's going on?"

"Now, Gunner!" I started the engine, and once he was inside the truck, I handed him the phone. "Keep your eyes on the screen and let me know what the fuck is going."

Doing as I asked, he looked down at my phone, and while I was heading through the gate, he gasped, "Holy shit!"

"What's happening?"

"Who is this chick?"

Unable to control my emotions, I growled, "Just tell me what the fuck is happening, Gunner!"

"From what I can tell, he's mouthing off about something, but she's acting cool. Doesn't look like she's bothered by what he's saying."

"How do you know that?"

"Cause she's smiling at him." He snickered. "Oh, shit. He must've said the wrong damn thing, cause she just Kung Fu'd his ass!"

I couldn't make sense out of what Gunner was saying. As hard as I tried, it just didn't make sense. Thinking I must've misunderstood, I asked, "She did what?"

"Dude, this chick is a badass! She just ninja chopped this motherfucker right in the damn balls, and now, the guy his holding his crotch and it looks like he's about to puke!" He was smiling ear to ear as he said, "Wow. I think I'm in love."

"Shut the fuck up, Gunner."

"Sorry, brother." The color drained from his face as he explained, "I just got carried away. I was all caught up in the moment and wasn't thinking."

Ignoring his explanation, I pushed, "What's happening now?"

"She just knocked this asshole off his feet, but he's trying to get up … Oh, damn."

"What?"

"Douchebag has a gun, Shadow." My heart started to pound so hard I thought it would come right through my chest when he added, "He's got it pointed straight at her."

Even though I was already gunning it, I pressed my foot against the accelerator as I raced towards the bookstore. "Keep talking, Gunner."

"He's talking to her, but I got no idea what he's saying." He paused for a moment, then said, "She's walking towards him. She's walking slow, and I can see her mouth moving. She's talking to him. Fuck. I wish I knew what the hell she was saying!"

"You and me both."

"Dude. She just keeps getting closer to this guy. What the hell does she think she's doing?" After a brief second, his eyes widened as he announced, "Damn it all to hell. She just plowed him in the side of the leg. Like, holy shit man. I'm pretty sure she just broke his fucking knee."

"Good. What about the fucking gun?'"

"I don't see it ... Wait! She's got it." I could see the surprised look in his eyes when he turned towards me and asked, "Who the hell is this chick, Shadow?"

"I'm beginning to wonder that myself."

"She's a friend of yours, right?"

"Yeah, but that doesn't mean I know every fucking thing about her."

"Hell, don't worry about it, brother. All women have their secrets. She just happens to have more than most." He looked back at my phone and said, "Damn. She's gone."

"What the fuck are you talking about?"

"Hold on ... How do you get to the other cameras?"

"Fuck. I don't know. Riggs didn't tell me."

As soon as I pulled up to the curb in front of the store, we both jumped out of the truck and rushed towards the door. When we walked in, we found the guy on the camera sprawled out on the floor, and he wasn't moving. Gunner nudged him with his foot as he asked, "Damn. Did she kill him?"

"Don't fucking care. I just want to know where the hell she is," I snapped as I headed towards the back staircase. "Keep an eye on him. If he moves, end him."

"You got it."

I'd gotten halfway up the stairs when Alex came barreling out of her apartment with two large boxes in her hands. Totally unaware that I was even standing there, she started down the stairs, but stopped cold when she almost ran into me. "Dammit, Shadow. You scared the living hell out of me."

"Where are you going?"

"It doesn't matter." She tried to inch past me, but I blocked her from passing. "Look, Shadow. I don't have time for this. Please move. I've gotta go."

"Not until you tell me what the hell is going on." I could see the wheels turning in her head as she considered her next move. When I saw a spark of determination flicker in her eye, I warned, "Don't even think about it."

She cocked her eyebrow as she asked, "Think about what?"

"Pulling that kickboxing shit with me." Realizing I knew about what had occurred with her unwanted guest, her eyes dropped to the floor. I reached out and took the boxes from her hands. "Just tell me who that guy is and why he's after you."

Her eyes locked on mine as she answered, "I've got some bad people after me, Shadow. That's really all I can tell you. It doesn't matter anyway. I'm leaving town, and you'll probably never see me again."

That thought didn't settle too well with me, and I found myself sounding more harsh than I intended when I replied, "You're wrong. It does matter—and you're sure as hell not leaving. Not like this. Not because of them."

"You don't understand," she cried.

"I understand more than you think." I lowered the boxes down on the step as I asked her, "Do you want to leave here?"

"Of course not, but I don't have a choice."

"There's always a choice, Alex. You could've chosen to go with that man tonight, but you didn't. You decided to fight, and that's what you have to do now. But this time, you don't have to do it alone. I'm here, so let me help you. Whatever this thing is, let me help you fight it."

ALEX

It was at that moment that I realized why I had been drawn to Shadow in the first place. Subconsciously, I knew he could handle anything that came his way, even my father and that he would protect anyone he cared for. As soon as I told him that I was in trouble, he didn't hesitate. He didn't weigh his options or consider the risk before offering to help me. I knew Shadow meant it when he said he would be there to help me fight. I could see it in the way he looked at me, spoke to me, and as much as I wanted to believe that he could, he didn't know my father, not the way I did. If I tried to stay, it would only be a matter of time before my father would find me, and once he had, he'd come after me. It was inevitable, and if I let Shadow get involved, there was a chance that he could get caught in the crossfire. I couldn't let that happen. If something happened to him, I would never be able to forgive myself, so whether I liked it or not, leaving town was my only option.

"I can't let you do that"—I knelt down and picked up

one of the boxes, then I tried to get past him—"but just so we're clear, I'm not just going to give up and accept my fate. I won't be going back there without a fight."

As I made my way around him, he asked, "Go back where, Alex?"

"Just leave it, Shadow. It's none of your concern."

He reached for my elbow and pulled me towards him as he argued his point. "If you're involved, then it is my concern."

"Why? Because you've had coffee in my store a couple of times or because we slept together?"

Fire flashed through his eyes as he replied, "You've got no fucking idea, do you?"

"How would I know what's going on in that head of yours, Shadow? You never talk to me. Hell, I don't even know your real name."

"Mason. My real name is Mason, and for future reference, if you want to know something, then all you have to do is ask."

"Well, thanks for the heads up, but it's too late now."

"If something is important to you, it's never too late."

"What exactly are you proposing here?"

"Come to the clubhouse. Let me and my brothers protect you from the people who are after you."

"I can't ask you to do that. It's not fair to you, and it's not fair to them."

"You didn't ask, Alex."

His mere presence was all-consuming, and having him so close was making it impossible for me to think. I was trying to come up with a viable reason why I couldn't accept his offer when one of Shadow's brothers appeared at the bottom of the steps. He looked up at us and shouted, "Hey, I hate to interrupt this little lover's quarrel you two have going on, but can I make a suggestion?"

"What?" both of us grumbled simultaneously.

"You seem to have yourself a nice setup here, and from what I can tell, you seem to like it here. So, why don't you just do like Shadow suggested and come back to the clubhouse with us for a few days? Give him and us a chance to help you get some of this shit sorted, and if it's something we can't see you through, then you can go. Then, when it's all said and done, you've bought yourself a little time."

I hated to admit it, but he was right. I needed a minute to collect my thoughts and make sure I was truly prepared to leave the city. I looked up at Shadow and said, "Okay. I'll go with you, but only for a couple of days."

Without responding, he picked up the second box and followed me downstairs. When we entered the bookstore, I was surprised to see that Berny was missing. As I locked everything up, I glanced around the room, searching for any sign of him. Shadow's friend must've noticed my concern and said, "Don't worry. I took care of him."

"Umm … okay." I had no idea what he'd meant by that until we walked outside. When we reached their truck, I spotted Berny in the back, bound and gagged, and he was still unconscious. I didn't know what they planned to do with him, and I honestly didn't care. I wouldn't mind if I never laid eyes on him again. When Shadow opened the passenger side door, I remembered that my car was still parked across the street. "What are we going to do about my car?"

"Where are the keys?" I reached into my pocket and pulled them out, dangling them in front of him. Shadow took the keys from my hand and then tossed them over to his friend and pointed to my car, which was parked up the street. "Follow us back over to the clubhouse."

With a quick nod, he turned and started towards my car. Seconds later, I found myself inside the truck with my belongings carefully stowed away in the back seat. I quickly glanced over at Shadow, and as I watched him pull out onto the main road, it hit me: By going to his clubhouse, I was about to enter the world of Satan's Fury —a place I never dreamed I would ever step foot in. Jason's earlier warnings came racing back to me, which made me even more anxious. Until that moment, I hadn't even considered that I could be rushing from the flame only to jump into the fire. I tried my best not to think about it and turned to look out the window. As I sat there staring at the people walking along the city street, I heard Shadow ask, "You okay?"

"No. Not really." I let out a deep breath as I said, "I'm just so tired. I knew this day was coming. I've tried to prepare myself for it, but now that it's here, I can't seem to think straight. I just want it to be over. I want to stop looking over my shoulder and just live my life."

His voice was low and tender as he asked, "Can you tell me what's going on? It would make it a lot easier if I knew what we were up against."

"I know, and I will. I promise, but can you give me a little time?"

"Yeah, I can do that."

"Thanks. I just need a minute to wrap my head around it all."

I felt the warmth of his hand on my thigh as he added, "I want you to know that you can trust me, Alex."

While I'd always liked the name I'd made up for

myself, hearing him call me Alex only made me feel worse. I'd just given Shadow a hard time about not telling me *his* real name, which was totally unfair considering I hadn't told him the truth about mine. I knew I should tell him, but I simply couldn't. I was scared. I was worried that Shadow would change his mind about me when he discovered who I really was, and I couldn't take that risk. He made me feel treasured and protected —and even if those feelings were just something I'd concocted in my head, I wanted to hold onto them for just a little longer. Without turning to look at him, I placed my hand on his and whispered, "I know I can, and thank you for that. Thank you for everything."

"Nothing to thank me for. I'm doing this as much for me as I am for you."

I was about to ask him what he meant but got distracted when we pulled up to a large metal gate. As it crept open, I leaned forward to get a better look at the clubhouse, and it was nothing like I'd expected. It was a beautiful, old brick building. "Is this the clubhouse?"

"It is."

"Wow. It's nothing like I would've expected. This place is amazing."

"I'm glad you like it. At one time it was one of the city's largest train depots." It was obvious that they'd done a great deal of work remodeling the lighting and some of the windows, but it still had that vintage vibe to it, making me feel a little less anxious about going inside. Once Shadow parked the truck, he turned to me and asked, "You ready?"

"I guess." Just as we were getting out of the truck,

Shadow's friend pulled up next to us in my car. "I need to get the duffle bag."

"I'll get it." Shadow walked over to the back of my car and shouted, "Hey, Gunner. Open the back door."

Once he'd grabbed my bag, he motioned for me to follow him inside. As we walked by the back of the truck, I noticed that Berny was no longer unconscious. "Um … What about *him*?"

Before Shadow could answer, Gunner replied, "I've got it handled."

"What are you going to do with him?"

"Do you really want to know?"

Realizing that I didn't, I replied, "Um … No. No, I don't."

"Didn't think so," he snickered.

When I saw that Shadow was already well ahead of me, I rushed over and followed him inside. As soon as I stepped through the door, I noticed the beautiful, ornate light fixtures that cast a serene glow along the long hallway. I wanted to stop and take it all in, but Shadow kept walking forward. As I followed behind him, I noticed how the dark wood and exposed brick gave the place a masculine feel to the décor, but it was perfect for such an old building. We passed doorway after doorway before finally stopping at one of the rooms at the end of the hall. I had so many questions floating around my head, but I kept them to myself—or at least I tried to. When Shadow opened the door and led me inside a large bedroom, I couldn't hold them back any longer. He tossed my duffle bag onto the king sized bed, and I asked, "What exactly is this place?"

"The clubhouse. Why?"

"I know it's the clubhouse, Shadow, but what's all here? Is this where you have your meetings, where you live, or just a cool place for you guys to hang out?"

"Yes, to all … at least for the most part. Not all of the brothers live here. Most of them have their own places, but each of them have rooms here for when they need them. There are also conference rooms, a playroom with TVs and stuff for the kids to mess with, and a full kitchen."

"Kids?"

"Yes. Kids. Like I told you, we are all family here. Many of the brothers have ol' ladies and kids, and some even bring their extended families by from time to time."

"Wow. I had no idea." I glanced around the room, making note of the large oak desk in the corner and the flat screen TV mounted on the wall. While it was a nice room with its own bathroom, there were no pictures scattered around, nothing of color or interest that made the room feel inviting. Instead, it felt cold, like it didn't belong to anyone. "So, whose room is this?"

"It's mine. It's not much, but it's home."

My eyes made their way back over to his bed—the bed where my duffle bag had landed, and I suddenly started to feel anxious. "So, um … where will I be staying?"

"In here … *with me*." He cocked his eyebrow as he asked, "That gonna be okay with you?"

As soon as the words slipped from his mouth, I glanced over to his king-sized bed, and my mind went to a place it had no business going, especially considering my present circumstances. I should've been focused on my father and the wrath he would bring when he discovered I'd slipped through his fingers, but I wasn't. In fact, he was the last thing I was thinking about as I answered, "Yes. It's more than fine."

He opened the drawer to his dresser and started moving things around. Once he made some room, he turned to me and said, "You can put your stuff here when you get ready."

"Okay."

"You want a hand?"

The adrenalin that had been pumping through me was starting to diminish, and I needed a minute to catch my breath. "No, thanks. I can do it."

"Alright. I'll leave you to it, then."

"Are you leaving?"

"Just going to check in on Gunner. I'll be right back," he assured me.

"Oh, okay." When he started for the door, I asked, "Do you mind if I take a quick shower?"

"Not at all. Help yourself."

"Thanks again, Shadow. I really do appreciate all this."

He walked over and gave me a brief kiss on my forehead as he replied, "You can stop thanking me, Alex. Really it's nothing."

With that, he turned and left the room, leaving me alone to sort through the mountain of thoughts racing through my head. After I grabbed a few clothes out of my bag, I headed into the bathroom and turned on the water. Once it was hot, I stepped inside, letting the warm water cascade down my shoulders. My mind drifted back to my father and the numbness I felt last time I saw him. The next thing I knew, the water had turned freezing cold and I was shivering at the bottom of the shower with my arms wrapped around my knees. I reached up to turn off the water, and my entire body trembled as I pulled myself to my feet. After drying off, I put on my clothes and dried my hair. Before heading back into the bedroom, I glanced at myself in the mirror and groaned when I noticed my red, swollen eyes. I'd tried to make myself believe that I was strong enough to handle anything, but as I stood there looking at my reflection, I started to have my doubts.

I wiped the last of the tears from my eyes and went back into the bedroom. Shadow still hadn't returned, so I went over to his dresser to start putting my things away. I'd just pulled the bottom drawer open when he came walking through the door. I glanced over at him, but quickly turned away when I remembered my puffy eyes. "Hey. You doing okay?"

"Yes."

"You sure about that?"

I closed the dresser drawer as I turned to face him. As soon as our eyes met, I knew he'd see that I'd been crying and I knew he'd want to know why. It meant a great deal to me that he cared, but I didn't want to talk about my father or anything else for that matter. I just wanted to escape in his arms and ignore the anxious feeling that was festering in the pit of my stomach. I needed to touch him, to feel his body against mine, and forget about the insanity that had become my life. There was no hiding my intent when I answered, "No. No, I'm not, and I need you right now… I need you to help me forget, even if it's just for a little while."

In just a blink, he was there, towering over me with a look of lust in his eyes that made me want him even more. I placed the palm of my hand against his cheek and said, "I don't know how much time I have. I just know I want to spend it with you."

His hand slipped behind me, pulling me close to his chest, and when I felt the warmth of his body next to mine, my world stopped spinning. His intoxicating scent, a mixture of cologne and leather, surrounded me, and when he leaned over and covered my mouth in a hungry kiss, everything else around seemed to fade away. The caress of his lips was pure magic. I felt safe in his arms, like nothing in the world could come between us, and for just a moment, I was able to consider the possibility that maybe there was something more happening between us than just fulfilling some carnal need. As he pulled me even closer and delved deeper into my mouth, I could feel his heart racing, and it was all I could do not to completely unravel in his arms.

He released my mouth just long enough to look down at me and say, "You gotta know that you deserve more than a man like me."

"No." My eyes locked on his as I whispered, "If you could see what I see when I look at you, feel what I feel when we touch, then you'd know just how amazing you really are."

"You're wrong, but I'm done trying to convince you. I want you, Alex. All of you," he whispered, the warmth of his breath caressing my cheek. I could see the longing in his eyes, the same longing I felt deep inside of me.

He studied me for a moment, searching for some kind of confirmation that I wanted this moment as much as he did, and once he found it, his mouth crashed against mine. We both let go of our doubts and just let ourselves get lost in the moment. The tips of his fingers trailed along my spine, and I arched towards him, seeking the heat of his touch. He continued to kiss me, and I could feel a fire burning deep inside me, smoldering as it spread through my body. The feeling only grew more intense when he reached for the hem of my t-shirt. As he pulled it from my body, I felt the palm of his hand linger over my bare flesh, making me shiver with anticipation. Unable to wait a moment longer, I lowered my hands to the waistband of my shorts, and with Shadow watching my every move, I lowered them to the floor.

His eyes roamed over me, and when I noticed the passion that lay behind those beautiful blue eyes, my pulse pounded harder, roaring in my ears as he inched closer. He ground his hips into mine, revealing his growing erection as the bulging denim ground against my center. Everything was happening so fast, but it felt like a dream, every detail playing out in slow motion. I wanted it so much. I wanted *him* so much, and I couldn't wait a moment longer. Groaning into his mouth, I eagerly unbuckled his belt and released him from his jeans. I reached for him, my fingertips gently brushing across his swollen shaft. I heard him take in a hastened breath as he reached behind me to remove my lace bra.

Once it hit the floor, his eyes dropped to my breasts, and he breathed, "So damn perfect."

"Mason…," I pleaded, stealing the last of his restraint. I gasped when he lifted me up, cradling me close to his chest as he carried me over to the bed. He held me tightly, making me feel safe and secure in his arms, then lowered me down onto the mattress. He stood over me, gazing down at me as he removed his clothes, and a rush of heat washed over me as he lowered himself onto the bed, covering me with the warmth of his body. His mouth dropped to the crook of my neck, and he began trailing kisses down my collarbone. When he reached my breast, he gently took my nipple in his mouth, taking his time as he nipped and sucked at my sensitive skin before lowering his mouth to the curves of my stomach. I groaned with anticipation when I felt him lower my panties down my legs before settling his head between my thighs.

My legs quivered as his tongue gently raked over my center. His touch was soft and gentle as he circled my clit, making my entire body tingle with need. While he continued to torment me with his mouth, he eased his fingers inside me, twisting and swirling as he found the spot that caught my breath. I loved how his hands felt against my skin, so strong and solid, and after just a few moments, I could feel my release approaching, causing me to whimper as my body tensed and filled with heat. When the sensation grew to be more than I could bear, I screamed out with pleasure, calling out his name over and over as my orgasm exploded, rocking me to my very core.

"Unbelievable," he rasped as he rose up to his knees. When I caught sight of his throbbing erection, I couldn't resist the temptation to reach for him. I took him in my hand, then slowly started to stroke him. A sense of satisfaction washed over me as I felt him grow even harder, urging me on as I moved my hand up and down his long, thick shaft. He shifted his body closer, and his eyes were trained on mine as I leaned forward and gently sucked the tip of his cock into my mouth.

"Fuck," he growled.

"Hmm," I moaned and opened my mouth wider. His hand dove into my hair, gently tugging as he silently begged me for more. When I took him in my mouth as far as I could, he tilted his head back and incoherently muttered my name. I loved seeing him so completely lost in the pleasure I was giving him. A low rumble worked its way through his chest when I started to move faster, licking and sucking his cock, making him struggle to maintain his control. I listened to his sharp breaths and watched the torment on his face until his eyes suddenly opened and locked on mine.

"Need to be inside you, Alex. Now," he growled.

He reached for his jeans, and I lay back on the bed, watching as he slid the condom down his thick shaft. Seconds later, he was settling himself between my legs. He looked down at my body with desire so intense I could feel the heat of his gaze burn against my skin, leaving no doubt in my mind that he wanted me just as badly as I wanted him.

SHADOW

Alex felt so damn good as she whimpered and moaned beneath me. As much as I wanted to savor the moment, remember the sound of her breath and the feel of her skin, I was already to the point of pure agony. I couldn't wait another second and drove deep inside her with one swift thrust. Her head flew back as she gasped at the sudden invasion which made my entire body still. I looked down at her, gazing upon her gorgeous, naked body, and I was completely captivated by her beauty. I'd never seen anything quite as magnificent as her lust-filled eyes locking on mine. I lowered my mouth to her shoulder, kissing her along the contours of her neck, and goosebumps prickled across her skin when the bristles of my beard tickled against her skin. It wasn't long before her hands trailed down my shoulders to my ass, pulling me towards her as she rocked her hips forward. I withdrew slowly, deliberately, causing her to groan in frustration as she waited for me to enter her again.

"Please," she pleaded as her fingernails dug into

my hips.

Answering her plea, I eased into her again, and as I increased my pace, she began to move with me, matching my demanding rhythm. I couldn't imagine a better feeling. I drove deeper, harder, and as she tightened around me, another deep moan vibrated through her chest. As we continued to move together, I could feel her body tensing beneath me, urging me on as I became more determined to bring her to the brink of ecstasy. I took her harder, faster, forcing her closer to the edge with every thrust. Alex's hands curled around my back as she braced herself for the next wave that crashed through her body.

"Come for me," I whispered as I slid my hand down between our bodies. No sooner had I brushed the pad of my thumb over her swollen clit, she came unglued. Her breath quickened as she clamped down around me, making me lose all of my self-control. She was so tight, so fucking wet. Having no other choice, I submitted to my own release and drove into her one last time, burying myself deep inside her as I came.

With great reluctance, I withdrew from her and laid down on the bed. As soon as I was settled, she curled up next to me and rested her head on my shoulder. We'd barely had a chance to catch our breath when there was a knock at my door, and Riggs called out to me, "Yo, Shadow. You in there?"

"Yeah. Give me a minute." I quickly got out of bed, and after I pulled on my boxers, I went over and opened the door. As soon as I laid eyes on him, I knew something was wrong. "What's going on?"

"Got something you need to see."

"All right. Just let me put on some clothes."

"Come down to my room when you're done, and you might want to let her know that you might be a while. Gus will be calling us all into church soon."

When Riggs turned to leave, I closed the door and reached for my jeans. As I started to get dressed, Alex cleared her throat and with a sly smile she asked, "So, you're running off on me again, huh?"

"Only because I have to," I answered as I eased my t-shirt over my head. "I'll make it up to you when I get back."

"Is that a promise?"

"I'll do my best." After I put on my boots, I went over to her and gave her a brief kiss on her forehead. "But only after we talk."

I watched as her eyes filled with doubt, making me think she might try to put me off again, but she surprised me. "Okay, but I'm going to warn you … hearing everything might change how you feel about me."

I didn't have time to tell her that she was wrong. There was nothing she could say that would change the fact that she'd turned my entire world upside down, and just to have her near made me feel things I didn't even know I could. She made me want more, and nothing would change that. Hoping it was enough for now, I told her, "Not a chance."

I kissed her once more, and then left to find Riggs. When I got down to his room, he was sitting at his desk with his eyes glued to one of his monitors. While it often gave me an uneasy feeling, I'd always marveled at what he could do with a simple laptop. As soon as he noticed me standing in the doorway, he motioned me over. "Come have a seat."

As I sat down next to him, I asked, "What's going on?"

"We got a name." He handed me one of the stacks of paper as he continued, "Rodrigo Navarro."

"So, Jasper talked?"

"Hell, he did more than that. He told Gus everything about this guy and more. I've just spent the past hour confirming what he's already told us."

"You gonna fill me in?"

"Navarro approached Jasper about a year and a half ago. At the time, he had no idea who Navarro was, but he was intrigued by the big wad of cash he flashed in front of his face. When he found out that the guy was just looking for information, he took the cash and told him everything he wanted to know."

"What kind of information was he looking for?"

"He wanted the names of anyone who was selling drugs in the area. It didn't matter if they were big or small, he wanted to know everything there was about them from who their suppliers were to which street corner they used. He took note of everything, and once he had what he wanted, he left, and Jasper didn't hear from him again … until a few months ago."

"That's when he hired him to start taking out our boys?"

"No, not yet. This time he wanted Jasper to find him a place to set up a meth lab, the kind that could generate a shit ton of product in a short amount of time. Sound familiar?"

"The Culebras?"

"The one and only." He crossed his arms as he leaned back in his chair. "Apparently, he was their distributor out in California, and he sent them here to get his new lab set up. He provided them with the location, supplies, and all the startup money they could possibly need, and all they had to do was deal with the competition. They thought it was a sweet deal until they crossed paths with us."

"Damn straight." As I thought back to the night that we blew up that meth lab, I remembered how the flames engulfed every member of the Culebra gang and left no trace of them behind. It was a well-deserved demise for the motherfuckers who'd killed two of our brothers. "You would think that alone would be enough for Navarro to steer clear of Memphis."

"Not a chance," Riggs scoffed. "This guy is used to getting his way, and he's not gonna stop until he gets it. That's why he's back. Jasper admitted that he paid him to kill off our boys, but none of that makes any fucking sense to me."

"Yeah, but Boone and Hoss told the same fucking story."

"Yeah. I'm not saying it isn't true. I'm just saying it doesn't make any fucking sense. I mean, come on. Think about it. This guy has the money and power to bring on one hell of a war, especially after we fucked up his plans for setting up production here, but all this guy does is pay Jasper to wipe out a few of our guys. Doesn't that seem odd to you?"

"So, you're thinking that he's got another plan in play, and he's just using Jasper as a distraction?"

"Honestly, I don't know what this guy is thinking, but something tells me that killing our boys was just the beginning."

"Then, let's take this guy out before he can cause any more damage." I looked around at all the stacks of papers that were scattered around his desk as I asked, "You got something here that might help us get to him?"

"I might, but I have to ask you something first." He paused for a moment, then grimaced as he asked "How well do you know Alex?"

I didn't like the tone of his voice, especially when asking about someone who'd quickly become important to me, and I found myself getting defensive as I answered, "I know her well enough. Why? What does she have to do with any of this?"

"Do you know anything about her past? Where she grew up? What she did before she started working at the bookstore?"

"What the fuck, Riggs? If you've got something on your mind, just say it."

Sensing my frustration, he held up his hands and said, "Hold on. I've got my reasons for asking."

"Then, get on with it."

"Jasper told Gus that Navarro had a daughter, and after doing a little digging, I came across this." As he handed me a piece of paper, he said, "This is her … Alejandra Navarro."

I was horrified when I realized it was an old photograph of Alex. I couldn't believe my eyes. Her hair was different and she was much younger, but there was no doubt that it was her. For the past year I'd only known her as Alex, the bookstore owner. I wasn't stupid. I knew she was hiding from something, that she had her secrets, but I never dreamed those secrets would include Navarro—the very man who was trying to take down Satan's Fury. "Damn. I can't fuckin' believe it's her."

"Yeah. This girl has gone to an awful lot of trouble to

wash her hands of Navarro. She cut all ties with her past, moved clear across the country, changed her name, and from what I can tell, she hasn't been in contact with her father in almost eight years. That's some pretty heavy shit for a teenager to handle on their own."

"You gotta wonder what drove her to leave?"

"There's a reason why Navarro has been so successful." Riggs handed me another stack of photographs mostly filled with some pretty gruesome images. "The guy's a cold-blooded killer who doesn't let anyone stand in his way. It couldn't have been easy living with a man like that. There's no telling what kind of hell she went through. She was lucky that she got away from him when she did."

"Well, I think her luck just ran out."

After I told him about everything that had happened at the bookstore with Alex and how adamant she was about leaving town, he said, "Fuck. So, what Jasper said was true. He *has been* looking for her."

"Yep, and apparently, he's found her … unless there was another reason that asshole attacked her today."

"Is she still in your room?"

"That's where I left her." My mind drifted back to Alex lying in my bed, and when I thought about how she'd felt in my arms, I wanted nothing more than to keep her close and protect her. Without me even realizing it, I'd fallen for her, and there was nothing I wouldn't do to keep her out of harm's way, even if that meant killing her father with my bare hands. I ran my fingers through my hair and let out a deep breath before saying, "Riggs … *this girl* …"

"You don't have to say anything," he interrupted me. "I already knew this girl meant something to you, brother. Hell, I'm pretty sure I knew even before you did."

"Then, you know I'm not going to let anything happen to her."

"Yeah, I know that, too."

"So, now what?"

"We talk to Gus."

He stood up and I followed him down the hall to Gus's office. When we walked in, he was sitting at his desk talking to Moose, but the conversation quickly ceased when they noticed us standing in the doorway. They both watched silently as Riggs and I took a seat next to Moose and remained silent as Riggs told him everything that he'd uncovered about Navarro. I could feel the tension radiating off of each of them as they listened to the news about Alex, making their silence that much more palpable. Once Riggs had informed them of everything we knew, including the fact Alex was actually on the premises, Gus was done listening. He leaned forward, placing his elbows on his desk, as he turned to me and asked, "You had no idea this girl was in trouble?"

"No. Not until that motherfucker showed up at her bookstore."

"What has she told you about her situation?"

"Nothing," I admitted shamefully. "She's kept this entire thing hidden from everyone. Hell, I don't even think Hallie knew who she really was."

"Then, it's time we hear what she has to say."

I nodded, then said, "I'll go get her, but Prez … we need to be careful with her. She's been through a lot, and trust isn't going to come easy."

"Don't worry, Shadow." With his eyebrow perched high, he assured me, "I can handle your girl."

ALEX

I'd always known there was a chance my father would find me, and I knew if that day ever came, he'd expect me to come back home. He would want me to go back to the way things were and forget about the new life I'd created for myself. I couldn't let that happen, so I tried my best to formulate a plan. At first, I thought I'd try to reason with him, explain how truly happy I was, and show him how successful I'd become, then maybe he would simply let me stay. But there was just one problem —my father wasn't a man who could be reasoned with —*ever*, so I had let go of that fantasy. I had to focus on the reality of my situation—my father was a cold, ruthless killer who would use any means necessary to bring me home. Having no other choice, I tried to prepare myself for the worst, thinking of all the different ways he'd make his appearance, and after going through scenario after scenario, I'd devised several plans for my grand escape, none of which included me ending up at the Satan's Fury clubhouse. And yet, there I was, lying in Shadow's bed trying to decide my next move.

As much as I wanted to believe that he might be able to help me, I couldn't expect him to take on my problems as his own. Dealing with my father would be dangerous, a life-on-the-line kind of dangerous, and it wasn't fair to get him, nor his brothers, involved in my screwed-up situation. While I hated the thought of leaving him, especially after the moment we'd just shared, I knew I had no other choice but to go. With great reluctance, I pulled myself out of his bed and put on my clothes. Once I was done, I collected my things and stepped out into the hall. I was relieved to find that there was no one around. Trying my best not to be noticed, I hurried towards the exit. Just as I was about to reach the door, I heard Shadow call out my name.

"Alex?"

Surprised by his sharp tone, I stopped dead in my tracks. Without turning to face him, I replied, "Just let me go, Shadow."

"Can't do that."

"Why not? It's the best thing for everyone concerned."

"You're wrong about that, *Alejandra*. In fact, you couldn't be more wrong."

I felt the air rush from my lungs at the sound of my name. There was only one way he'd know that name, the name that connected me to my father and all the lies I'd told. As I slowly turned to look at him, I tried to brace myself for the anger I expected to see on his face. Only I didn't see anger, nor anything like it. Instead, there was that same look of longing I'd seen in his eyes just a few hours earlier. Thinking I must've misheard him, I asked, "What did you say?"

As he continued walking towards me, he replied, "I know everything, Alejandra."

"You do?" I asked with my voice trembling with surprise. "Then, why are you trying to stop me from leaving? Aren't you furious with me for lying to you?"

"Not exactly happy about it."

"Then, why wouldn't you want me to just walk out that door and never come back?"

He was just inches away from me when he answered, "Because I don't want you to go."

"But why?" I couldn't believe my ears. After discovering the truth about my past, I thought he'd hate me, but there he was telling me to stay. I simply didn't understand. I knew I was pushing him to say things he might not be ready for, but at that moment, I needed him to tell me exactly what was on his mind. "This is something I need to know, so you're going to have to explain what's going through your head, or I'm walking out that door."

He inhaled a huge breath and slowly released it with a deep-seated growl. After several long, torturous moments, he answered, "I never thought I'd find someone who could make me feel the way you do, and now that I've found you, I'm not just going to let you walk out that fucking door. Is that enough of an explanation, or do you need more?"

"Um … that will do for now."

"Good." He slipped his arm around my waist and pulled me close as he leaned down and pressed his mouth against mine, kissing me so deeply, so passionately, that my knees started to buckle. Nearly losing my balance, I let my duffle bag drop to the floor before wrapping my arms around him and melting into his arms. I relished the feeling of security when I was close to him, and even though I was terrified by it, I wanted it more than anything else in the world. Just as I was getting lost in the moment, he took a step back, releasing me from our embrace, and as he reached down and picked up my bag, he said, "Gus wants a word with you."

"Gus?"

"He's the president of the club."

"Wait … the president of Satan's Fury wants to talk to me? About what?"

I felt like the rug had been pulled out from under my feet when he answered, "Your father."

"He knows about my father, too?"

"He knows everything that I do, Alex, but there are some things that you don't know … things that only he can explain."

"I don't understand."

"You will."

He motioned for me to follow as he headed back to his room. After dropping my bag off in his room, he led me down another long hallway and my stomach twisted into a knot when we entered a large office. I was only expecting to meet Gus, the notorious leader of the Satan's Fury, but when we stepped inside the room, three, big, burly bikers were sitting there waiting for us. They turned and looked at us, and the way they looked at me made me feel like a tiny rabbit surrounded by three hungry wolves. I wanted to get the hell out of there, run and never look back, but then, I felt Shadow's hand drift to the small of my back and suddenly my racing heart started to calm.

The older man sitting behind the large, wooden desk with his thick, salt-and-pepper goatee and dark, brooding eyes eased back in his chair and smiled as he said, "Her pictures don't do her justice, Shadow. I can see why she caught your eye."

Before Shadow had a chance to respond, the large man sitting directly in front of the desk, stood up and motioned me over to his seat. "It's nice to finally meet you, Alejandra. I'm Moose, the VP of the club. The fella behind the desk is our president. You can call him Gus, and I think you've already met Riggs."

"It's nice to meet you as well … *all of you,*" I replied as I walked over and sat down. I was too nervous to even think about small talk, so I said, "Shadow mentioned that you wanted to talk to me about my father."

"Hmph … Straight down to business. I like a girl with spunk." Gus chuckled. "But yes … I would like to hear more about your story, including your father. We know ya left California eight years ago. Cut all ties with your family. Changed your name. Met up with Hallie and ended up at the book store. What I don't know is … why?"

"Is this sudden interest in my father because of me or something else?" I asked boldly.

"Both, but we will get to that later. Right now, I want to know how you ended up here in Memphis."

"I've got plenty to say where he is concerned. I'm guessing you want to know more than just the fact that he's a horrible human being, so I'll tell you what I know, and we can go from there."

I spent the next twenty minutes telling him everything I knew about my father, and I was amazed by his reaction or better yet, his lack of reaction. He didn't seem surprised by anything I told him. Hell, he didn't even bat an eye when I told him about my mother. It was like he expected something like that from him. I wish I had been so intuitive to know what a monster he could be, but I couldn't fathom something so horrific coming from my own flesh and blood. Once I was done, he said, "I can't imagine how difficult that must have been for you. It had to be hard, even harder to get away from him. How did you pull it off for all these years?"

"You're right. It was hard. It took months of planning." I sighed as I thought back over those months of anguish. "It was just a few days after Christmas when I heard him talking about my mother. After that, I knew I had to get away from him. I pretended like everything was normal right up until the day I left for college, but nothing was normal. I was filled with hate and anger, and that's what kept me going. I managed to get a new social security card, a fake id, and everything else I'd need to disappear. Since I'd paid my tuition to USC in advance, I was able to get a refund when I withdrew. I used that money to get out of town. I traded my car and left for Memphis. That's when I met Hallie. You know the rest."

"Hmmm. Smart girl."

"I was desperate." I shrugged. "I would've done anything to get away from that man."

"Can't say I blame you there," Moose scoffed.

"So, now you understand why I can't go back there." I looked up at him as I said, "But please know … I never intended to bring my problems to your doorstep, and if you want me to leave, I'll go right now. I would certainly understand."

"Your father has been looking for you for years, right?"

"Apparently."

"How did he find you?"

"A photograph was taken of me during a concert at one of the local bars. He used that to track me down. I'm guessing he sent Berny to bring me back home."

"Is that the guy you tangled with at your book store?"

"Yes, sir."

"I gotta say, it was pretty impressive the way you handled him."

I smiled as I replied, "Marcus trained me well."

"Marcus?"

"He was one of the men who worked for my father, but he was one of the good ones. He was always looking out for me." I thought back to his visit and groaned when I remembered the envelope he'd given me. "He actually came to warn me that my father was coming for me. I should probably let him know what happened."

"Sorry, doll, but I can't let you do that. In fact, I need your cell phone and any other devices you might have on ya?"

"But why?"

Riggs turned and answered, "Because they can use them to track you. It will be even easier now that they know you're here in Memphis."

"Damn. I didn't know they could do that."

"Not many people do, but don't worry. Riggs will take care of it." He leaned forward with a serious expression on his face as he said, "I know today hasn't been easy for you, Alejandra and I don't want to add to that, but the club needs your help."

"My help? With what?"

"Dealing with your father." I could see the concern in

his eyes as he explained, "Your father might be a heartless sonofabitch, but he's smart. He's spent his life making his business what it is, and now, he's got his sights set on Memphis."

I couldn't hide the surprise in my voice when I asked, "You know why I don't want him here, but why is it such a big deal for you?"

"Because his presence here endangers everything the club has worked for, and I can't let that happen." He paused for a moment before continuing, "Your father has to be dealt with before it's too late, but he hasn't been an easy man to track down. That's where you come in."

"So, you want me to help you bring down my father?"

"Yes." Before I could give him my response, he added, "But, let me be clear. I know you are important to Shadow, and that makes you *important to me* and all the brothers of Satan's Fury; so no matter what you choose to do here, we'll help you any way we can."

Without hesitation, I answered, "I'll do anything you want me to do."

"I need you to be sure about this."

"I'm sure," I assured him. "After what he did to my mother, he deserves whatever he has coming to him and more. I just need to know what you want me to do."

"Glad to hear you say that." He ran his hand over his thick goatee, slightly tugging on the end as he said, "Now, we just have to come up with a plan to draw him out, and then we can take things from there."

"That should be easy enough. Just use me as bait." The thought of seeing my father again made my blood run cold, but I knew it was the best way to get him to come forward. "I can reach out to him and tell him that I'm ready to come home."

I couldn't even finish my sentence before Shadow stepped forward, and the room fell silent when he growled, "*No fucking way.*"

"But …"

"No buts, Alex. I'm telling you now, there's no way in hell that's gonna happen."

SHADOW

No one wanted Navarro taken down any more than I did. After all he'd done to my club and to Alex, there was nothing I wanted more. If given the chance, I'd wrap my fingers around his fucking throat and squeeze the life right out of him. Better yet, I'd spend a few hundred hours showing him the kind of pain that only a man like me could dish out. I just needed him within my reach, and then, he'd be finished, once and for all. We all wanted to be done with Navarro's bullshit, but using Alex to flush him out wasn't an option. While I knew she was willing to do anything to help bring her father down, just the thought of having her in harm's way made my stomach turn. I couldn't let that happen, but I could tell from the look on her face that she wasn't going to give up on the idea.

Her voice was strong and full of determination as she said, "Whether you like it or not, using me is the best way to get to my father, especially now when he's so adamant about getting me to come back home."

"There's got to be another way."

"I may not know much about how my father runs his business, but I do know that he's a man who doesn't like to lose. Right now, he's got his focus on winning me back. It only makes sense to use that to lure him out. Besides it's not like you won't be close by to make sure I'm safe."

Gus looked over to him and said, "She's got a point, brother."

"There's no way in hell that he's going to believe she's suddenly changed her mind and is willing to come back home," I argued. "He'd have to know that it was a trap."

"What if I gave him a good reason for changing my mind?"

"And what exactly would that be?" I roared. "You've said yourself that your father is a smart man. He's not going to buy into some bullshit that you've suddenly had a change of fucking heart and you are giving up your life here to go back home to him! There's no way he'll ever believe that, especially after what happened earlier today. Once he sees that his guy didn't make it back with you, he'll know something is up and he'll plan accordingly. You try this bullshit and there's no doubt that he'll turn the tables on you. Then, what are you going to do?"

Her eyes dropped to the ground as she mumbled, "Oh, well. I uh … I hadn't thought about that."

Gus could see that I was becoming irritated, so he interrupted our dispute by saying, "Hold on, you two. We're not getting anywhere like this. We need to take a step back and clear our heads. Why don't you take her back down to your room, and we can discuss this more in the morning?"

I nodded, then reached for Alex's hand and led her out

of the office. I'd let my frustration get the best of me, and I tried to collect myself as she followed me back to my room. Unfortunately, I wasn't having much luck calming the storm of emotions that were raging inside of me, mainly because I'd never experienced anything like it before. I wasn't a man who had these kinds of feelings, and I had no idea how to deal with them. I glanced over at her, and I could see the concern in her eyes as we stepped into my room. She stopped, and without saying a word, she turned and looked at me, waiting for me to speak. I had so many things I wanted to say to her, but I just wasn't ready. I needed a moment to ground myself, so as I walked past her, I said, "I'm going to take a shower."

"So, you're not going to talk to me about all this?"

"I need a minute, Alex," I growled. "Can you give me that?"

She shrugged her shoulders and waved her hands with sass as she rolled her eyes and spat, "Take all the time you need."

Ignoring her sarcasm, I walked into the bathroom and started my shower. I removed my clothes and stepped under the hot water, letting it soothe the tension in my shoulders. While I didn't understand the feelings I had for Alex, there was no denying that they were there. At first, I thought it was just a needed distraction, that seeing her helped make the shadows of my past less daunting, but that in itself proved that this thing between us was more than just an attraction. She was more than that, much more, and as fucked up as it might be, it took me seeing her in danger for me to realize that. That was enough for me to know that I wasn't good enough for her, but I no longer cared. Selfish as it might be, Alex was mine, and I couldn't stand the thought of her being in danger. I would do everything in my power to protect her, even if that meant protecting her from herself.

After I got out of the shower, I wrapped my towel around my waist and stepped back into my room where I found Alex already in bed. She was curled up on her side with her back to me and she lay completely still as I dropped my towel and slipped into bed next to her. I slipped my hand around her waist as I eased up behind her, and while she didn't resist, she didn't acknowledge my presence. She just quietly stared ahead. I knew I should say something, tell her what I was feeling, but the words just wouldn't come. After lying there for several moments, she finally asked, "Are you going to tell me why you are so mad at me, because I really don't understand what I did wrong. I was just trying to come up with a way to help ..."

"I'm not mad at you, Alex."

"Then, what's wrong?" Her voice trembled as she asked, "Was I right? Did hearing about my past change things for you?"

"No, Alex. Nothing has changed for me." I lowered my mouth to her shoulder and slowly trailed kisses along the curve her neck. "From the moment I first laid eyes on you, I knew nothing would ever be the same for me."

"How did you know that?"

I paused for a moment as I tried to think of the best way to explain it to her. "For as long as I can remember, I've lived in darkness, seeing nothing but shadows around me, but when I'm with you ... I see everything. I see the light, the colors, and the shadows are no longer there."

With tears in her eyes, she rolled over, and as she faced

me, she placed the palm of her hand on my jaw. "As crazy as it may sound, I feel the same way about you. I didn't even realize what I was missing until you came along."

I lowered my mouth to hers, kissing her softly. While it wasn't my intent, the kiss quickly became demanding and full of hunger. I wanted her, needed her, and my hands became possessive as I pulled her body close to mine. As soon as our bodies touched and I felt the warmth of her skin on mine, there was no way I could resist having her. Without removing my mouth from hers, I eased on top of her, slowly lowering her lace panties down her legs before settling myself between her thighs. We spent the next few hours making love, and once we were both completely sated, she nestled in the crook of my arm and drifted off to sleep. As I looked down at her, studying the delicate lines of her beautiful face, I realized I'd finally found it. The one thing I thought I would never find—*love*. I had fallen for her, hard and heavy, and there wasn't a damn thing I could do about it. Trying my best to accept my new found realization, I closed my eyes and submitted to my own exhaustion.

When I woke the next morning, I was a bit dazed and confused. For the first time in years, the nightmares hadn't come. I'd actually slept through the entire night with no memories flooding my dreams, and as I glanced over to Alex nestled by my side, I knew it was because of her. She alone had kept them at bay, giving me my first night of freedom. My chest tightened at the thought, and I found myself even more captivated by her. I lowered my mouth to her forehead, gently kissing her, but she didn't budge. The night had taken its toll on her, and I decided to let her sleep. I carefully eased out of bed, trying my best not to disturb her as I got dressed and left to find Gus. Just as I stepped into the hall, Blaze called out to me.

"Gus just called us all into church."

Curious why he'd call us in at this hour, I asked, "Something going on?"

"Yeah, but won't know what it is until we get down there."

"Damn."

When we got down to the conference room, Gus and Moose were already sitting down, and they watched as the rest of us quickly filtered into the room. As soon as we were settled, Gus stood up and said, "I know you all have been anxious to hear what's been going on, but I wanted to wait until I had all the facts before I brought you all together. That's no longer an option, so I'll tell you everything we know thus far."

Gus spent the next twenty minutes updating the brothers on everything we'd learned about Navarro. The tension in the room crackled around us as he explained his connection to the Culebras, and his reasons for sending them here. Emotions were running high as we all thought back to Runt and Lowball's death which only ran higher when Gus announced, "You all know that he used Jasper to take out four of our men, and while that's bad enough in itself, we've recently discovered that he's stepping up his game."

"How's he doing that?" Gunner asked.

"He tried hacking into our database ... but Riggs managed to side rail him by setting up dummy accounts that we can use to send him fabricated intel."

Gunner smirked as he said, "That a boy, Riggs."

"Don't start celebrating just yet, Gunner. Turns out

Navarro was able to put a tracking device on one of our SUVs, and from what we can tell, he's been tailing us for weeks ... even more. To make matters worse, if he was tracking our last run, there's a possibility that he's monitoring Ronin as well."

"Fuck," Murphy growled. "How in the hell did he find out about him?"

Ronin was our main distributor, and he was an invaluable asset when it came to our pipeline. Once we gathered the shipments from the other clubs, it was up to us to deliver the goods to him in Baton Rouge. As soon as we got everything to him, he'd load it on one of his barges and make sure they got to their final destination. The fact that Navarro might have managed to get intel on our connection with Ronin was a huge hit to the pipeline. It was clear that Gus was concerned when he said, "I've got no idea, but I intend to find out."

Tank asked, "So, how are we planning to take this motherfucker down?"

"I'll tell ya, it's not gonna be easy with this guy, but we might just have the upper hand." He turned and looked at me as he said, "Turns out he's got a daughter—Alejandra Navarro. The story is she ran away from home eight years ago, and since then, he's been searching for her. It just so happens that we found her first."

My back stiffened when Blaze asked, "We gonna use her to draw him out?"

"I wish it was that simple." He let out a deep breath as he explained, "It just so happens that Alejandra changed her name to Alex Carpenter and has been living here in Memphis. Some of you already know that she has a connection with Shadow, and when trouble came knocking at her door, he brought her over to the clubhouse for our protection."

"He also brought one of Navarro's men along with her. He might be able to give us some additional intel on Navarro," Gunner suggested.

"Absolutely."

"Have you spoken with the daughter?"

"We have, and she's willing to do whatever she can to help us."

"If she's willing to help us out, then what's the problem?" Blaze pushed.

"The problem is me," I growled. "I protect what's mine, and I'm not putting her in danger."

Knowing her stance on the matter, Riggs argued, "And what does she have to say about it?"

"It doesn't fucking matter what she says. There's no way in hell I'm going to put her in jeopardy."

"Ease there, brother. You gotta have a little more faith in us than that. We can use her without putting her life in jeopardy, Shadow," Blaze argued.

"If you can guarantee me that she won't get hurt … that he won't touch a hair on her head, then and only then will I agree to use her."

"Consider it done," Gus announced. "We won't pursue this until we can come up with a plan we can all agree on."

"I'm good with that." I thought back to Jasper and asked, "What do you want to do with Jasper and the others."

"They knew what they were doing when they went against Fury," he growled. "I say end 'em."

I couldn't agree more, so I answered, "Consider it done."

"What about the run?" Gauge asked. "We gonna hold off until we track down Navarro?"

"I'll talk to Cotton, but consider the run still on. I think it's time to turn the tables on Navarro and give him a taste of Satan's Fury."

As soon as we were dismissed, everyone dispersed, going in their own direction as they considered everything they'd just been told about Navarro. Over the next few days, he became the main topic of all our conversations, and every time his name was mentioned, I found myself becoming more and more wound up, especially if Alex's name was brought into the discussion. I wanted to do everything I could to protect her, and as I climbed into bed with her each night, I found that feeling growing stronger. When I was close to her, the demons that raged inside of me were silent, including the nightmares. For several nights they hadn't come, and for the first time in years, I'd been able to sleep without the memories of my past gnawing at me to remember the things I wanted to forget. Unfortunately, the peace was short lived. With all the talk of Navarro, I found myself seeping into the darkness, and after a long, excruciating day at the garage, I was beyond exhausted. I crawled in the bed next to Alex, and I'd only been lying there a few moments when I felt a feeling of dread wash over me.

I'd been living in the Ridley house for just over four years, and I was feeling completely defeated. I'd tried telling Mrs. Haliburton what was going on with the Ridleys many times, but she never believed me. The other kids in the house, including Michele, always denied that anything was going on, and when I tried telling my teachers at school, they'd just end up telling Mr. Ridley what I'd said, causing him to lose his mind and beat the hell out of me as soon as we were alone. I'd finally given up on getting help and decided to accept my fate, but it wasn't easy, especially when I knew what he was doing to Michele. I wanted to find a way to make it stop, but any time I tried to intervene, I only made things worse.

I was sprawled out on my bed, staring at the ceiling, when I heard the familiar sound of his footsteps creeping up the stairs. My entire body grew tense when I heard him open Michele's door. Everything stilled around me as I rolled to my side and tried not to think about what was going on, but when I heard a strange thud, I found myself climbing out of bed. I walked over to my doorway and froze. As I stood there, I thought about how much I hated what was happening, and rage started building inside of me. I couldn't take it anymore. I was determined to end this once and for all, and I charged towards Michele's room and slammed my shoulder into the door, causing it to burst open.

Mr. Ridley was on top of Michele and had her hands pinned down at her side, and I nearly gagged at the sight. When he finally realized what I'd done, he sprang off of her and rushed towards me. "You've got some nerve coming in here again. You're done, boy!"

I ducked when he took a swing at me and plowed my fist into his stomach, causing him to stumble backwards. "I won't let you hurt her anymore!"

Once he regained his footing, he charged at me again, this time slamming his shoulder into my chest as he pinned me against the wall. Even though I'd grown bigger and much stronger over the past few years, he still had a good hundred pounds on me, making it difficult to break free from his hold. "I don't know why I didn't end you a long time ago."

With his hand clenched firmly into a fist, he nailed me in the ribs, over and over again. He had me in a position where I could barely move, so I did the only thing I could. I reared back and crashed my head right into his nose, causing him to flail back. When his hands reached up for his nose, I rushed towards him, wrapping my arms around his waist as I tried to tackle him to the ground, but my efforts were in vain. I couldn't get him off his feet, and in a matter of seconds, he was back on me. Hoping that she might be able to help, Michele came up behind him, tugging at his arm, as she cried, "Please, just stop. Leave him alone."

Ridley threw up his arm, shoving her out of the way. She stumbled, and with her hands extended in my direction, she fell backwards, hitting her head firmly against her bedside table before collapsing on the floor. There was something about the way her body fell limp that didn't seem right, and I knew I had to get to her. Once I broke from Ridley's grasp, I rushed over to Michele. Her eyes were open, but she didn't acknowledge me as knelt down beside her. I reached for her, but stopped when I saw the blood pooling around her head. My heart started pounding in my chest so loudly that I couldn't hear anything else. I knew it was bad, but I just couldn't make myself believe it. I gently shook her, hoping for some kind of response, but got nothing.

She was gone.

ALEX

After spending several days at the clubhouse, I realized that there was a great deal more to the brothers of Satan's Fury than just the crazy rumors I'd heard. If they were, in fact, vicious killers who were doing unspeakable things, they certainly had me fooled. I knew they had their secrets, that they did some unspeakable things, but from what I could tell, they seemed like good, decent men who put their brotherhood above all else. Even though my father was causing the club all kinds of trouble, they'd been nothing but kind to me. Each and every one of the brothers made me feel welcome and part of their family.

During the day, most of them were busy dealing with club stuff, but during those brief moments I'd shared with them at breakfast or dinner, I'd enjoyed getting to know each of their different personalities, including Shadow's. The more I was around him, the more I understood my initial attraction towards him. While he was often quiet and reserved, it was the little things he would do that showed his compassionate side. Not only was he thoughtful of me, he never hesitated when one of his brothers came to him for help, and even though he didn't cut up like Gunner and T-Bone, there was a softer side to him—a side that I'd come to love. He seemed to sense when I was feeling uncomfortable or out of place, and he'd place his hand on my thigh or give my hand a light squeeze, letting me know that he was right there with me.

The more time I spent with the brothers and their ol' ladies, the more comfortable I became with all of them, including the club girls who were clearly surprised by my presence. I chose to ignore their questionable stares and spent my time watching the dynamic between the brothers. It gave me a much needed distraction from the anxious feeling I had in the pit of my stomach. I enjoyed those moments of reprieve, because when I was alone, I became consumed with worry. I'd find myself thinking about my father and just how far he'd go to find me. Those thoughts terrified me, and I wasn't alone. Shadow was also concerned.

While he hadn't actually said the words, I could see it in his eyes whenever he looked at me. I wanted to ease his mind and assure him that everything would be okay, but there was no way I could know how things would turn out, especially when it came to my father. I knew the club was planning to use my help to get to him, but I had no idea what they had planned. They'd put everything on hold until they'd returned from their trip to Louisiana. The not knowing what was to come was difficult, but I tried to have faith that they would figure things out. I wanted to talk to Shadow about it, but knowing he was totally against me being involved, I decided to leave it alone. I thought I would let him deal with his doubts on his own, but I changed my mind when he started having another horrible nightmare. Like the night before, he hadn't been sleeping long when he started mumbling in his sleep. While I couldn't make out what he was saying, it was clear that he was distraught. Sweat started to bead across his forehead as he thrashed from side to side, and when I tried to wake him, he became even more agitated.

"Mason! Wake up," I whispered as I nudged his side. When that didn't work, I shook him a little harder and said his name a little loud. "Mason! You're having a nightmare. Wake up!"

He gasped as he sat up in the bed, and when he finally opened his eyes, he let out a deep breath. After a moment of gathering his senses, he finally turned to me and said, "I'm sorry. I thought they'd stopped."

"You thought what had stopped?"

"Nothing," he answered as he laid his head back down on the pillow. "It was nothing."

"That wasn't *nothing*, Mason."

"It was just a dream."

"But …" I started, but stopped when he threw the covers back and got out of bed. When he started putting on his clothes, I asked, "Where are you going?"

"You know we have the run today. We'll be heading out soon."

I glanced over at the clock, and when I noticed that it was only four-thirty in the morning, I said, "But it's so early."

"I don't know what to tell you." I could tell he was becoming aggravated when he snapped, "I've got shit to do."

"*You tell me* what the hell is really going on with you." I eased off the bed and walked over to him. "I know this thing with my father and me is bothering you, but you haven't talked to me about it. I feel like you're shutting me out, and I don't know what to do about it."

As he pulled his shirt over his head, he answered, "I'm not shutting you out, Alex."

"Then, talk to me. Tell me about the nightmares."

"You. You're the only thing that's on my mind," he snapped. "Every minute of every fucking day, it's *you*."

I stepped towards him, and as I placed the palms of my hand on his chest, I told him, "I know you are worried about the club using me to get close to my father, but I trust them and most of all, I trust *you*. Together, you will find a way to make this work. You'll see."

"I won't let anything happen to you, Alex."

"I know that. You just have to believe."

He leaned towards me and kissed me lightly on the forehead before he said, "I've gotta get going."

"If this thing us between is going to work, you can't keep shutting me out. You have to find a way to talk to me."

"I will, but not today. I've gotta go."

"Fine." As he started towards the door, I told him, "Be careful."

"Always."

He closed the door behind him, leaving me alone once again. Since it was still so early, I crawled back into bed and tried to go back to sleep. After a great deal of tossing and turning, I finally managed to doze off. Several hours later, I woke up to the sun trickling in through the curtains. I glanced over at the clock and saw that it was almost eight. I stayed there for several more minutes, but when my stomach started to growl, I eased out of bed and started to get dressed. I'd just gotten on my clothes when I heard someone knocking. I opened the door and found Riggs standing in the hall with my laptop and a cell phone. "I thought you might need these. I transferred all of your contacts to the burner, so you are all set."

As he handed them over to me, I said, "So, they're safe to use now?"

"Yep, you're all good. Just be careful about who you call and what you say. You don't want to take any chances."

"Okay. I will. Thank you so much!"

"No problem."

When he turned to leave, I asked, "You aren't going with the others?"

"Yeah, we're just about to leave now."

"Oh … umm … have you seen Shadow?"

It was obvious from his expression that my question had caught him off guard. "No, but I'm sure he's just been getting ready for the run. You want me to let him know that you're looking for him?"

"No. That's not necessary. I was just curious."

"All right then. I'll see ya when we get back."

"Okay. I hope it goes well."

When he turned to leave, I closed the door, then took my laptop over to Shadow's desk and turned it on. I tried to log into my email, but when I realized that my account had been deleted, I closed it and reached for the cell phone Riggs had given me. I scrolled through the contacts that had been added, and stopped when I came across Jason's name. As I sat there staring at his number, I was overcome with guilt. I hadn't spoken to him in days, and knowing he must be worried, I dialed his number. It rang several times before he finally answered, "Hello?"

"Hey, Jason. It's me, Alex."

"What the fuck, Alex? Where are you?" he roared.

"I … uh." I hadn't actually thought things through and struggled to find the right words to say to him. "I had to go out of town for a few days."

"You should've called and told me something! I didn't know what to think. Hell, I was about to contact the police!"

"I'm really sorry. Things got really hectic, and I forgot to call."

"Whose phone number is this? I've been calling yours for days and haven't been able to get anything but your voicemail."

"I lost mine and had to get a new one."

"Well, are you okay? I've been going out of my mind worrying about you."

"Yes. I'm fine. I'm really sorry that I worried you, but an emergency came up and I had to leave unexpectedly."

I could hear the concern in his voice when he asked, "What kind of emergency?"

"Just a family thing … I'll explain it all to you later. I just wanted to let you know that I was okay."

"When are you coming back?"

"I'm not sure just yet. I'll call you when I figure things out."

"Is there anything I can do?"

"No. This is something I have to do on my own."

"Are you sure? What about the bookstore?"

"I don't know what I'm going to do about that. For

now, I will just have to keep it closed. I don't have any other choice."

"Why do I get the feeling you aren't telling me something?" he pushed.

"Because you are a worry-wart who always assumes the worst. I'll be fine, and as soon as I get back, I'll explain everything."

"What about ..."

Before he could finish his question, I said, "Jason, I've really got to go. I'll be in touch when I can."

I hated being so cryptic, but the last thing I wanted was for him to get involved in this mess with my father. I had no choice but to hang up the phone and pray that he wouldn't do anything stupid. As I sat there going over everything in my head, I felt my stomach rumble with hunger. While I didn't have much of an appetite, I knew I needed to get something to eat, so I put my phone down and headed to the kitchen to find something to settle my stomach. On most mornings, you could hear the guys bantering back and forth as they ate their breakfast, but it was oddly quiet as I stepped into the kitchen. After I made myself a bowl of cereal, I went over to the table and sat down. I'd just started eating when I heard someone walk in. I turned and saw a beautiful brunette wearing hospital scrubs covered in bright colored balloons coming towards me.

She smiled as she said, "Hey! You must be, Alex."

"I am." I returned her smile as I replied, "And you must be Blaze's fiancé."

"That I am." She extended her hand to me as she said, "My name's Kenedee. It's great to finally meet you."

As I shook her hand, I couldn't help but stare. She was

quite beautiful, and with her hair pulled back in a ponytail, she looked so young and innocent, making me wonder how a woman like her ended up being with a man as fierce as Blaze. "It's nice to meet you, too. I've heard a lot about you."

She went over to the counter, and after she poured herself a cup of coffee, she came over and sat down next to me. "Yeah, I bet you have. These guys always have some story to tell."

"That they do. Sometimes I have to wonder if they are all true."

She laughed as she replied, "Oh, they're true. They might exaggerate here and there, but they're all true."

"Oh, wow. That's a scary thought."

"At least they've lived to tell about it."

"That's very true." I giggled. "So, how did you meet Blaze?"

Her face lit up at the sound of his name. "We first met down at Daisy's, the club's diner. He helped me get my food out to my car, and then we met again when his son was admitted into the hospital where I work. He asked me out, and I guess the rest is history."

"I remember Blaze telling me that you worked at the trauma center. Do you like working there?"

"It gets a little intense at times, but I love it."

"It's great that you love your job like that."

"Yeah. I couldn't imagine doing anything else." She took a sip of her coffee before asking, "You own a bookstore, right?"

"I do. It was actually Hallie's. She was a close friend of mine, and she left it to me when she died last year."

"Oh, I hate to hear about your friend. She must've been special to leave you the bookstore."

"Yes. She was very special to me, and I still miss her dearly. I think about her every morning when I open the store."

"I can imagine." I could hear the curiosity in her voice when she asked, "You met Shadow there, right?"

I couldn't hold back my smile when I answered, "Yeah, but it took me forever to actually talk to him. You know, he can be a little intimidating."

"Hmm … yes. Yes, he can." She laughed again. "I have to admit, I was a little surprised when Blaze told me that Shadow was seeing someone."

"Really? Why is that?"

"Well, like you said, he can be a little intimidating, and he's not a big talker."

"No, he's definitely not, but he says a lot with only a few words."

She studied me for a moment, then smiled as she asked, "How are you adjusting to things around here?"

"I don't know. Pretty good, I guess. I'm still getting to know everyone, but I think it's going okay."

"I know it can be overwhelming. I still remember my first few days. It was an adjustment for sure, especially with all the different rules."

"Rules?"

"You mean Shadow hasn't talked to you about it?"

"No. Not really."

I could see the surprise in her eyes when she answered, "Oh."

"With everything that's been going on, we really

haven't had time to talk about it. So, what are these rules you're talking about?"

"I think that's something you should discuss with Shadow."

"Well, he's not here, and you are," I pushed. "Just give me the gist of it, so I'll have an idea of what I'm dealing with."

"Okay, but you're gonna have to hold on. I'm gonna need more coffee for this."

Once she's refilled her cup, she came back over to the table and immediately started sharing the ins and outs of the club. She seemed surprised by my lack of reaction when she explained that club business was never discussed with the women, and she seemed even more surprised that I wasn't bothered by the fact that we weren't supposed to ask questions. It might've seemed strange to her, but over the years, it was something I'd grown used to. My father never shared his business dealings with me or my mother, and neither of us ever questioned him—about anything. It simply wasn't done. Furthermore, I'd spent the past eight years doing everything I could to keep my identity a secret, and I knew the consequences that would occur if it ever got out. Knowing how detrimental it could be, I understood why the brothers of Satan's Fury kept their secrets. It was their way of ensuring their family's safety, and I didn't begrudge them for doing so.

SHADOW

I got an uneasy feeling when we pulled up to the dock in Baton Rouge, one the largest ports in the area. At this time of day, you'd normally see people scurrying around as they prepared their next shipment, cranes high in the sky, shifting from one side to the other as they loaded their cargo onto the different ships, and barges creeping down the river as they made their way down south. But as I surveyed the area, I was surprised to see that it was completely deserted. There was no one in sight for miles, not even out on the water, and the fact that Ronin and his guys weren't there to meet us wasn't a good sign. From day one, they'd always been there to give us a hand and keep a lookout. It took a good deal of effort to unload all the crates from the two horse trailers, especially when they had to be removed from the secret compartment that was hidden beneath the horses' feet. Once we'd gotten all the crates out of both trailers, they'd help us carry them over to the storage container on the barge. Even though Ronin knew Gus's plan and that today's shipment wouldn't be like the others, I still expected him to be there when we arrived. Seeing that he wasn't, I could only assume that Navarro had read Riggs' dummy email and had used the information that was provided to know exactly when and where our run would be.

Knowing there was a strong possibility that we had visitors, Murphy and I instructed the others to stay put while we checked things out. I eased the truck door open, and as soon as my foot touched the gravel, I knew we had eyes on us. I could sense it, and when I glanced over at Murphy, it was clear from his expression that he felt it, too. It wasn't like we hadn't expected company. After talking to Berny, Navarro's man who tried to kidnap Alex, we knew Navarro had managed to put a small tracking device on one of the club's SUVs. While we had no idea how long it had been there, we knew he had used it to gather intel on Fury, including our connection to Ronin. It was a definite hit to the club, but we hoped we could use it to our advantage. Instead of immediately removing the tracker, we left it alone, hoping to provide Navarro with misleading information.

As we continued towards the door to Ronin's warehouse, the hairs on the back of my neck stood tall, making me stop dead in my tracks. I slowly turned, and as I scanned the building to our left, I spotted something glimmering in the distance. I knew from experience that the light came from the sun reflecting off the lens of a gun scope.

"We've got company. Two o'clock," I warned Murphy as we continued towards the door. "I have a feeling we'll have more inside."

"Um-hmm. Also have one at five o'clock and nine."

"Damn." Just as he was about to reach for the door handle, I said, "Hold up, Murph. We got no idea what's waiting for us on the other side of that door."

"Maybe not, but we sure as hell know what's waiting for us out here." With his weapon in hand, he pulled the door open and said, "They already know we're here, so there's no reason for us tiptoeing around."

Realizing he was right, I positioned my AR on my shoulder and followed him through the door. Once we were inside, we found Ronin and two of his men sprawled out on the floor. They were all bound and gagged, leaving no doubt that we weren't alone. When I crouched down to check on him, Ronin nodded his head forward, letting us know that our guests were still close.

Murphy reached for the mic on his headset and whispered to Blaze, "We just found Ronin."

After a few seconds, he ordered, "Yeah. Look alive, brother. They're closing in."

He'd barely had a chance to hang up the phone when gunshots exploded around us, forcing us both to take cover. We hunkered down behind several metal cargo carriers and the warehouse instantly became eerily quiet. My heart raced, but not with fear. It was moments like these that made my adrenaline kick in, giving me a rush like none other. I lived for times like these, and as I watched as Murphy peeked around the corner, I found myself feeling eager for the battle to begin. I got my wish when he spotted one of the shooters approaching on our left. He pulled his trigger, and we both heard a loud thud when the guy hit the ground. Anticipating another round of shots, we remained in our positions for several more minutes. I had no idea what was going on outside, and just the thought of my brothers being in danger made it impossible for me to wait a moment longer. I stepped out from behind the shelter of the cargo carrier, and with my AR aimed straight ahead, I advanced forward, searching for our next victim. Worried for my safety, Murphy hissed, "Dammit, Shadow!"

"I'm done with this shit," I growled.

Everything seemed to be moving in slow motion as I charged ahead. With each step, I took in every shape, every smell, and every sound; it wasn't long before something drew my attention to several large barrels that were gathered in the back corner. As I moved closer, I could see the outline of a dark figure cowering behind them. Like the others, he was dressed in all black with a balaclava hat covering his face. Without a moment's hesitation, I pulled the trigger, killing him instantly.

I continued to comb the area, and once I thought the room was clear, I went over to one of the windows to check on the others. Unfortunately, I couldn't see a damn thing through the dirt and grim, so I used the butt of my gun to bust the dingy glass, giving myself a better view of the parking lot. When I peeked through the open hole, I noticed two men standing on top of the building. I aimed and quickly took my shot, killing one of them instantly. I was just about to take out the second man, when I heard a gunshot behind me, followed by a burning sensation in my upper arm. "Fuck!"

Before the asshole could take another shot, Murphy came up and shot him from behind. When he noticed my arm, he asked, "You okay, brother?"

I looked down at my wound, and once I saw that it was just a graze, I answered, "Yeah, I'm good."

When we turned our attention back to the window, we could see several men headed towards our trailers. I looked over to Murphy and said, "Make the call."

Murphy used his headset to radio over to Blaze and ordered, "Now!"

We both watched anxiously as Blaze and the others stood up, revealing themselves from their hiding spots inside the two trailers. They quickly positioned their weapons in the small, side windows and began shooting round after round. Within seconds, they had killed everyone in sight, leaving the parking lot scattered with bodies. Once I felt certain that the others were safe, I went over to release Ronin and his men. After I took my pocket knife and cut the zip-ties that restrained their hands and feet, I helped Ronin up off the floor. He rubbed his wrists as he said, "Is everyone okay?"

"Not sure just yet. We need to go check on the others."

They all followed me to the back door, and when we stepped outside, several of the brothers were gathered around Gunner. As we got closer, I noticed the blood splatter across his left shoulder. One of the prospects handed him a towel, and as he held it tightly against his shoulder, he shouted, "I can't believe I got shot … *again*! It's like I have a fucking target on my back!"

Blaze went over and took a look at his wound. "Oh, come on, brother. It's not that bad. The bullet went straight through."

"That's easy for you to say. You're not the one who just got shot!"

T-Bone walked over next to Blaze, and as he looked

down at Gunner's wound, he said, "Blaze is right, man. It's a clean shot. Mack will be able to fix you up as soon as we get back to the clubhouse."

"Well, clean or not, the motherfucker hurts like a bitch," he complained.

"Stop pouting, Gunner. Women are impressed by battle scars," Blaze snickered.

"I don't need help impressing the ladies, asshole."

Blaze would've taunted him all afternoon if Ronin hadn't come over and interrupted them. "We need to clean this mess up before the cops show up. With all the shooting, there's no doubt somebody called them."

"I'm on it," Murphy assured him, then turned to us and started dishing out orders. As soon as he was done talking, we all started gathering Navarro's men and loaded them into the back of one of the horse trailers, leaving no sign that we'd even been on the premises. Just as we were about to leave, Ronin turned to Murphy and asked, "So, what's the plan from here?"

"Everything's on hold. You're gonna need to torch the warehouse and find a new location for future drop-offs." Murphy's tone turned stern as he said, "You've got to go invisible, brother. Gus isn't gonna be happy about how things played out today."

"That shit isn't on me, Murphy," Ronin growled. "It was your guy who let him put a tracker on one of your fucking SUVs!"

"And you're the one who let him get past your security and almost got yourself killed. You knew there was a possibility that he would show up here today, and you weren't prepared. That shit is on you."

It was clear that Ronin wasn't happy with Murphy's

response, but he knew what he said was true. Ronin had never once dropped the ball, but when it counted most, he'd let the club down. Thankfully, we were prepared and were able to take up the slack. Ronin ran his hand through his hair and sighed. "You're right. I underestimated that motherfucker."

"That you did. If you plan to continue working with us, you're gonna have to step up your game. Use this time to set up a new location and improve your fucking security."

"I'll take care of it."

"I have no doubt that you will. Now, let's get the fuck out of here before we end up with more trouble on our hands."

With that, we all started loading up. Gunner crawled in the backseat of our SUV and laid down. After taking some pain medication, he just wasn't himself, and he didn't spend the six-hour drive home yammering about a bunch of nonsense. Instead, he closed his eyes and tried to ignore the throbbing in his shoulder. It was clear that he was in pain, so as soon as we pulled into the city limits, Murphy put a call in to Mack, letting him know that Gunner and I would need medical attention when we arrived. Realizing we were getting close, Gunner sat up and watched silently as we pulled up to the clubhouse. As soon as we were parked, Gunner and I went inside and headed straight for the med-room. Since it was so late, I was surprised when I spotted Alex walking in our direction. She smiled when she first saw us, but her expression quickly changed when she noticed the blood that stained our clothes.

"Oh, my God! What happened?" she screeched as she ran over to us.

"We ran into a little trouble, but we're fine, Alex. Don't worry."

"Are these gunshot wounds?"

"Just a couple of battle scars, doll," Gunner smirked. "Nothing we can't handle."

While I was amused by Gunner's change of attitude, Alex was not. She was consumed with worry, and I could hear the anguish in her voice as she asked, "Did my father have something to do with this?"

"We'll talk about that later. Right now, I need to get Gunner down to see Mack. He needs to look at his wound."

"And yours?"

"Mine's just a graze, baby. I'm fine," I assured her.

"I still want him to check it out."

"All right. I'll have him take a look. Why don't you go back to the room?"

With a look of determination, she demanded, "No. I'm going with you."

Seeing that she wasn't going to take no for an answer, I reached for her hand as I led her down the hall to the med-room. When we walked in, Alex stopped and her mouth dropped open as she looked around the small infirmary. There were cabinets on either side of the room that were filled with various medical supplies, and several gurneys were lined up in the center of the room. Knowing we were coming, Mack had already set up one of the stations and was waiting for us when we walked in. When he saw Gunner, he couldn't help but tease him for being shot again. "I wasn't expecting to see you back here so soon."

"Trust me, I'm just as surprised as you are," Gunner groaned. "I'm just hoping it's not going to set me back like last time."

Mack used medical shears to remove Gunner's shirt, and Alex gasped when she got a look at his wound.

I placed the palm of my hand on her back as I whispered, "Don't worry. It looks worse than it really is. He's gonna be fine."

After Mack checked him thoroughly, he announced, "Looks like Murphy was right. It was a clean shot. You got lucky, brother."

"So, no surgery?"

"No. I don't think that will be necessary. Just a good cleaning, a few stitches, and you'll be set to go."

Sounding relieved, Gunner replied, "I'm good with that."

Mack looked over to me and asked, "What about you? Is the wound deep?"

I shook my head. "No, it's just a graze."

"Let me have a look."

Alex watched as he used the shears to cut a slit in my sleeve and grimaced when she saw the burned line of bleeding flesh on my upper arm. While it could've been worse, it was a gruesome looking wound. She bit her bottom lip as she tried to keep it together. Mack finally said, "Might need a couple of stitches."

"It's fine, Doc. Just give me the stuff to clean it up and a couple of bandages. You take care of Gunner."

Mack nodded, then turned to get all the supplies I'd

need. Once he'd set them down beside me, I reached for the antiseptic, but Alex took it out of my hand. "I'll do it."

While Mack started working on Gunner, she reached for a cotton swab and carefully dabbed the solution on my wound. It burned like hell, but I didn't show any sign of discomfort, hoping that it would ease her anxiety. Unfortunately, that didn't happen. As she continued to work on my wound, I noticed tears building in the corner of her eyes, and it pained me to see that she was upset. "It's okay, Alex. I'm fine."

"That's not the point. I know you deal with this sort of thing all the time, but this time, it's my fault that you are here."

"How the hell is any of this your fault?"

"I should've stopped him. I should've just gone home and convinced him ..."

Before she could finish her thought, I reached for her hand, pulling her close to me as I whispered, "No, Alex. None of this is on you. There's nothing you could do or say that would've changed any of this. Deep down, you have to know that."

"But, I could've tried." She looked up at me with determination as she said, "I couldn't take it if something happened to you. I have to try to end this thing, Shadow."

"And how do you plan to do that?"

ALEX

When it comes down to it, all you have is strength and hope. Hope that you can get through the tough times to find your way to the good, and the strength to keep it together until you get there. I was holding onto both as I followed Shadow down to Gus's office. After seeing both Shadow and Gunner come back with actual gunshot wounds, I knew I couldn't stand by and let my father continue on his path of destruction. I had to try to find a way to convince him to let go of his plans to destroy the brothers of Satan's Fury and move on to his next target. If he refused, I'd use all the strength I could muster and use what Marcus had taught me to find a way to kill him myself. I simply couldn't let him cause the brothers anymore harm. It wasn't going to be an easy task. He'd set his mind on winning, and I knew he wouldn't walk away without feeling like he'd come out ahead. I hoped that by going home to him and being the daughter he always desired me to be, it would be enough to satisfy his lust for victory, but more than that, I hoped I'd have the strength to see it through. Leaving Shadow and the life I'd created for myself would be the hardest thing I'd ever done, but one way or another, I had to stop my father before it was too late.

As soon as we walked into Gus's office, he looked over to Shadow and asked, "How's the arm?"

"Good. Not much to it."

"Sorry, but I don't agree," I argued. Even if they'd both survived the attack, Shadow and Gunner had been shot, and I couldn't take the chance that it would happen again. "This has to stop. I need to talk to my father and end this thing once and for all."

"Not sure that's a good idea."

"You have to know that I'm the only one who is going to be able to get through to him."

His eyes narrowed as he replied, "I don't disagree, but after what transpired today, I think we need to give it some time."

"Don't you see … It's only going to get worse from here? You have to let me do this before anyone else gets hurt," I pleaded.

"And just how do you plan to do that?" Gus pushed.

"I'll tell him the truth." I glanced over at Shadow as I said, "I'll tell him that I'm involved with one of the men of Satan's Fury, and that I will come home if he promises to end this feud between you."

"You're not going back there, Alex," Shadow growled.

"No, she's not," Gus agreed. "But, if she can get him here, then we'd get our chance to get close to him."

I tried to keep my voice from trembling as I said, "I can

tell him that I want to meet with him face to face to discuss my offer. If I can get him to agree, then you can take it from there."

I could see the tension in Shadow's shoulders begin to ease as he pondered the idea. After several moments, he finally said, "If we do this … if she goes to meet this asshole, I want every brother there to ensure her safety. There's no way in hell he's taking her anywhere, and if he lays a hand on her, he's dead."

"Agreed." Gus turned his attention to me as he said, "Make the call and keep it brief. You don't want to give him any reason to doubt your motives."

"Understood." As I pulled my phone out of my back pocket, I looked over at Shadow. I could see that he was apprehensive, so I placed my hand on his as I assured him, "He won't hurt me."

"I'm sure your mother thought the same thing."

His words stung with truth, making me even more nervous as I dialed my father's number. I hadn't called that number in over eight years, and as it began to ring, my chest started to tighten with fear. I knew I had to make Gus and Shadow believe that I was just using myself as bait, that I really wasn't planning to leave with my father, so I had to watch my words. Everything I cared about was counting on that one phone call, and if I didn't pull it off, I could lose it all. My heart skipped with horror when my father answered, "Yeah?"

"It's me. Alejandra."

There was a long pause before he replied, "Alejandra? Is that really you?"

"Yes, dad. It's me." I paused for a moment, then said, "I need to see you."

"Is that so?" he asked with suspicion. "Then, why haven't you come home? If you were here, you could see me any time you wanted."

"That's what I wanted to talk to you about."

"What's there to talk about?" he clipped. "Your place is here with me where I can take care of you and keep you safe."

"Safe? You mean, like you kept my mother safe?" I snapped. As soon as the words slipped from my mouth, I knew I'd screwed up, but I just couldn't help myself.

"What are you talking about?"

Trying my best to get the conversation back on track, I answered, "I have something I'd like to discuss with you. It's important. It's something I need to say in person. Will you come talk to me?"

"There's nothing to discuss, Alejandra."

"That's where you're wrong. We have a lot to discuss."

"Like what?"

"I know you want me to come home and you're willing to do whatever it takes to get me there, but have you thought about how things are going to be once you have me back."

"It will be like it used to be. We will be a family again."

"You know I don't want that, so how are you planning to keep me from leaving? Are you going to watch me every second? Lock me away ... keep guards on me every minute of every day just so you can make sure I stay put? Is that the way you want things to be, or would you rather me come willingly and be the trophy daughter you've always wanted me to be?" I gave him a moment to consider the thought before I continued. "I'll be the daughter you want, but it will come at a cost."

"And what is that?"

"Meet me. Talk to me face and face, and I will explain everything."

There was a long, agonizing pause before he finally answered, "Fine. I'll be at your apartment tomorrow morning at nine."

Nine was just a few hours away. I was worried that Gus and the others wouldn't have time to prepare, but I felt I had no other choice but to agree. "Okay. I'll be there."

"*Come alone,* Alejandra. There's no reason for things to get messy."

"I will. You have my word," I lied.

"Good. I will see you soon."

As soon as he hung up, I turned to Gus and said, "He'll be at my apartment at nine."

Gus nodded. "We'll be ready."

I let out a deep breath as I looked over to Shadow and said, "I need some fresh air."

"I'll go with you."

"That's okay. I won't be long," I told him as I started out the door. I rushed down the hall and out the front door, and I was practically running as I headed towards the back of the lot. Once I'd stopped, I placed my hands on the fence, clinging to it as I thought back over my conversation with my father. Tears started to stream down my face as I remembered the sound of his voice, and the hatred it stirred inside of me as he spoke. I detested everything about him, and the mere thought of having to face him again made my stomach turn. Nausea crept over me, and before I realized what was happening,

I felt the bile burning at the back of my throat as I hunched over. I tried to fight it, but I couldn't stop myself from getting sick. I was still bent over when I felt a hand run across my back.

As he reached for my hair, pulling it away from my face, Shadow asked, "You okay?"

I wiped my mouth, and after several deep breaths, I stood upright and nodded. "Yeah. I'm better now."

When I turned to face him, he said, "You don't have to do this."

"I know I don't, but *I need to do this.* Please don't try and stop me."

Without responding, he reached for my hand and led me back into the clubhouse. When we got back to his room, I went into the bathroom and brushed my teeth. Once I was done, I went back into his bedroom and found Shadow waiting for me on the edge of the bed. I sat down next to him, and neither us spoke for several minutes. Finally, he said, "You asked me about the nightmares."

Surprised that he'd brought them up voluntarily, I turned to him and said, "Yes ... what about them?"

"I've had them since I was just a kid," he admitted.

"Do you know why you have them?"

He nodded. "They're my mind's way of making sure I don't forget."

"Forget what?" I pushed.

"Occasionally, I'll have a dream about my time in Afghanistan, but mostly, they're about the years I spent in foster care."

"Did something happen while you were there?"

"Yeah, you could say that." He paused for a moment,

then ran his hand through his thick hair. "Janice and Cal weren't exactly the loving, doting type. They were both alcoholics who liked to use the kids as punching bags, especially me. Cal was also a fucking pervert who got off on raping the oldest girl in the house, Michele. She was only ten years old when it started."

"Oh, my God. That's awful." A part of me had always known that he had a tragic past, but I never dreamed it would be so terribly horrific. My heart ached for him as I told him, "I can't imagine going through that, especially after losing your parents the way you did. It must've been so hard for you."

"Yeah, but it was worse for her." I could hear the agony in his voice as he said, "I tried to make it stop, but everything I did just made it worse. No one believed me until the night he killed her."

"He killed her?" I gasped.

He lowered his head and sighed. "It was an accident. I'd gone in to her room to stop Cal from raping her for the hundredth time. I was fifteen at the time and thought I was strong enough to take him on. I was wrong. Michele tried to help, but when she did, he pushed her, causing her to fall backwards. She hit her head and never woke up."

"Oh, Shadow. That must've been terrible for you to witness as a child."

"It was the most difficult thing I've ever faced."

He'd finally let me in, and for the first time, I understood the darkness that dwelled deep inside him. I wished there was a way to erase his pain, but it had become a part of him, making him the man he was today. Hoping to learn more about his past, I asked, "What happened to your foster father?"

"One of the neighbors heard the argument, and for the first time in four years, they actually called the police. Both parents were arrested, and all the children were removed from the home. Cal was sent to prison and Janice was put on probation."

"They both deserved much worse than that."

"Cal got his in the end." He looked over to me as he said, "I looked him up a few months after I'd patched in the club and found out he'd been murdered by one of his fellow inmates. While I never asked, I'm pretty sure that Gus had something to do with that."

"Do you feel like you missed out on getting your revenge for what he'd done to you and Michele?"

"There are days when I think it's one of the reasons why I've had such a hard time letting it go, but in the end, it doesn't matter. He got what was coming to him."

"Then, why do you think you're still having these nightmares?"

"She died because of me."

"What?"

"If I hadn't gone in that room … if I'd just come up with another way, then she'd still be alive."

"You did everything you could, Shadow. You were just a kid. There was no way you could stop him."

"I could've made her run away with me. I could've put a bullet in his head. I could've …"

"No. You have to stop doing this to yourself." I got off the bed and knelt down in front of him. I looked up at him as I placed my hands on his face. "You aren't the one to blame."

"Maybe not, but I'll never be able to forgive myself for what happened." I shrugged. "It's one of the reasons I became the club's enforcer. I wasn't able to protect her the way I should, so now I'm doing whatever I can to protect my brothers. I guess you could say it's my way of finding some sense of redemption."

"What exactly does an enforcer do?"

"Let's just say that I use *any means necessary* to ensure my family's safety." An intense look crossed his face as he said, "I wish I would've done the same for Michele."

While I was curious to know more about his position in the club, I knew the nightmares he was having were more important, so I asked, "Do you think she would forgive you for what happened?"

"I don't know." I gave him a moment to consider my question, and eventually, he mumbled, "Yeah. I guess she would. She was never one to hold on to things, but I'm not her."

"So, you think I'm to blame for all the things my father has done … that I should've found a way to stop him … that it's my fault that you were shot today?"

"Our situations are completely different, Alex."

"I don't agree. I think they are very much the same." I leaned towards him and briefly kissed him on the lips. "I think you and I are very much the same."

Before he could respond, Riggs knocked on the door and said, "It's time."

"I'll be right out." He helped me to my feet as he stood up and started for the door. "I'll be back in a couple of hours."

"Where are you going?"

"We're going to check things out at your apartment. We want to make sure we're prepared for your father, but T-Bone will be around if you need anything."

"Oh. Okay," I replied, unable to hide my worry. Before he turned to leave, I said, "Please be careful."

"You know I will." As he opened the door, he turned to me and said, "Just hang tight and I'll be back as soon as I can."

After he was gone, I crawled into bed and tried to settle my racing heart. Even though I was exhausted, I couldn't begin to sleep. I was only a few hours away from seeing my father again, and I was finding it difficult to keep it together, especially after everything Shadow had shared with me. He'd finally opened up to me, making my decision to leave with my father even more difficult. I knew the brothers were trying to find a way to trap him, kill him even, but I knew he'd never let that happen. He was too smart to let someone undermine him, not even his own daughter. I had no choice. I had to go with him. It was the only way I could protect Shadow and the others. I'd have to give up my life to save his, and I'd do it without a moment's hesitation. I loved him with all my heart, and there was nothing I wouldn't do to protect him.

After spending several hours trying to prepare myself for what was to come, I finally decided to get up and get dressed. I pulled myself out of bed, and I was about to head into the bathroom when I heard my cellphone ringing. Thinking it might be Shadow, I rushed over and grabbed it off the desk. When I looked down at the screen, I was surprised to see that it was Jason calling. It was way too early in the morning for him to be calling, so I quickly answered. "Do you have any idea what time it is?"

"I need you to come over to my place." His voice was filled with panic as he said, "I need you to come now."

"Why? What's going on?"

"There's a man here. He says he's your father, and ..."

Before he could finish his sentence, a moment of static came through the line. Seconds later, I heard, "Hello, Alejandra."

My blood ran cold at the sound of my father's voice. I was stunned, confused, and found it nearly impossible to form a complete thought. I had no idea how my father found Jason, but the fact was, he had. "What's going on? Why are you with Jason?"

"I'm surprised at you, Alejandra. I thought my own flesh and blood would be smarter than this."

"I don't know what you're talking about."

"You really think you could pull a fast one over on me?" he hissed. "You think you can get yourself wrapped up in that fucking biker club, and I wouldn't find out about it?"

"But how did you know?"

"You were seen last night, my precious daughter ... outside by the fence."

My heart sank as I remembered the nauseous feeling I'd felt after speaking with him on the phone. I'd hoped that the fresh air might help the queasy feeling, and I'd run outside. My chest tightened when I thought back to Shadow coming out to check on me, and I was appalled by the fact that we were being watched. "What does any of this have to do with Jason?"

"You have half an hour. If you aren't here by then, I put a bullet in his head."

"And if I do?"

"Then, I let him go ... and if you come willing and alone, I'll end my strike against Satan's Fury."

"Do I have your word on that?"

"You do."

"Then, I'll come, but please don't hurt Jason," I pleaded. "He has nothing to do with any of this."

"Your time is running out, Alejandra."

"I'm on my way."

SHADOW

I knew what it was like to love someone with all of my heart only to lose them. It had happened to me twice, first with my family, and then with Michele. It nearly broke me, and after everything I'd been through, I thought I was destined to be alone, that love just wasn't in the cards for me. I accepted my fate without contention, but all that changed when I found Alex. I wanted to spend the rest of my life with her, and I wasn't going to let anyone, especially her piece of shit father, take her away from me—*not this time*. This time, I wasn't taking any chances. My brothers and I would be ready for Navarro, and if he so much as made a move towards Alex, I'd put a fucking bullet in his head. As I took one last look around her apartment, I felt certain that we'd thought of everything. Riggs had set up several backup cameras that were battery operated that we could use to monitor Alex even if Navarro managed to kill the power. The brothers had hidden themselves in different locations throughout the area, including her apartment, the roof and neighboring buildings.

Once we were certain that we'd left no stone left unturned, Riggs came over to me and asked, "You ready to go get her?"

"Ready as I'll ever be."

"Take a breath, brother. We got this. We won't let anything happen to her," he tried to assure me.

"I know, but I can't shake the feeling that we've missed something."

"Not a chance. We've gone over everything multiple times. And with the additional cameras, I'll be able to track her every move."

"It's not her that I'm worried about." I took another quick glance around her apartment before saying, "We better get going. I want to make sure we have plenty of time to go over everything with her before he gets here."

Riggs nodded and followed me down the stairs to our SUV. Once we were both inside, I started the engine and headed towards the clubhouse. My mind was running a mile a minute as I drove out onto the main road. Since none of us had any idea how this would all play out, I tried to think about every possible scenario, making sure we were prepared for anything that might happen. I thought we were prepared for anything, but I was wrong —very wrong. As soon as we got to the clubhouse, I went to my room to find Alex, only she was no longer there. Thinking she might've gone to grab a cup of coffee, I rushed to the kitchen, and once again, there was no sign of her. The uneasy feeling I had at Alex's apartment started growing stronger as Riggs and I searched the clubhouse for her. None of the brothers had seen her, including T-Bone who was just across the hall.

Since his door was propped opened, I was hoping that he'd know where I could find Alex. "Have you seen Alex?"

"She's not in your room?" he asked sounding surprised.

"Come on, T-Bone. Think," I growled.

"Fuck, man. I don't know. I haven't seen her, and I've been sitting right here since you left."

I looked back over to Riggs and asked, "Where the hell could she be?"

"Let me see if I can find her using her phone." He quickly turned, and I followed him down the hall. As soon as we got to his room, he rushed over to his computer and started typing. Seconds later, he looked over to me and said, "Looks like she got a call about an hour ago."

"From who?"

"A guy named Jason Brazzle. Got any idea who that is?"

"He's a friend of hers, but I don't know much about him. How long has it been since he called."

"It was just over an hour ago." He went back to typing and seconds later, he announced, "I got her. It looks like she's heading over to his place."

"What the fuck? This doesn't make any sense. She knows what's about to go down, there's no way she'd just leave without …" I ran my hand over my face as I tried to collect my thoughts, and then it hit me. "Goddammit!"

"You think her father is behind this?"

"He's gotta be. There's no way she'd just leave without talking to me first."

"Then, we better get our asses over there before it's too late."

As we raced out the door, Riggs put a call in to Gus, letting him know what was going on. Having no way of knowing if it was just some kind of trap, Gus ordered T-Bone and Gauge to follow us over to Jason's place. My heart hammered in my chest as I pressed my foot against the accelerator, racing towards the address Riggs had given me. I tried to gain control of my panic, but nothing was working. I knew it was just a matter of time before she was in her father's grasp, and I wouldn't be there to protect her. Guilt and anger consumed me as I parked across the street from Jason's apartment. As we got out of the SUV, Riggs looked over to me and said, "It's apartment 302, so I'm guessing we need to head up to the third floor."

As we started towards the front door, I noticed T-Bone and Gauge waiting for us in the alley. I motioned for them both to follow, and with our weapons drawn, we headed inside. Trepidation swelled through me as we made our way up the stairs. I kept expecting to come across one of Navarro's men, but there were none in sight, making me even more anxious as we approached Jason's door. Riggs leaned towards the door, trying to see if he could hear anything on the other side, and after just a few seconds, he nodded. Navarro was there. I took a quick glance around, and when I saw that there was no other way for us to get inside, I gave T-Bone the signal to knock the door down. With one swift kick, the wood splintered into a thousand pieces, giving us access to the apartment. We charged inside, but immediately froze when we saw a tall, dark skinned man with his gun pressed against Navarro's temple.

He seemed completely unfazed by Navarro's three men who had their guns pointed directly at him, and didn't so much as acknowledge our presence as he snarled, "I'm not letting you do this … not after what you did to her mother."

Navarro's face filled with repulsion as he growled, "I always knew you were in love with her, Marcus. Hell, anyone could see it. *So fucking pathetic.*"

I quickly scanned the room and was overcome with relief when I spotted Alex huddled in the corner with her friend, Jason. He looked like hell as he leaned against her with his arm across her shoulder. His eyes were nearly swollen shut, and bruises and cuts covered his face. Someone had given him one hell of a beating, and from what I could tell, Alex was the only thing keeping him from falling on his face. When Alex's tear soaked eyes locked on mine, it was all I could do to keep from rushing over to her. I knew she was distraught, but at the moment, there was little I could do to console her.

"She was too good for you. She deserved better, and you know it."

"Maybe, but that doesn't change anything. She's still dead, and there's nothing you can do about it."

"But, I can keep you from doing the same thing to Alejandra." He pressed the barrel of his gun into Navarro's flesh as he replied, "I can still protect her."

"You're making a mistake, Marcus. If you pull that trigger, you're as good as dead."

I remembered Alex telling me about Marcus. He was the man who'd trained her how to fight, and as I stood there watching him put his life on the line for her, I quickly realized just how much he must've cared about her. She must've realized it, too, because she started to cry when she heard him say, "I don't care. I'd rather die than let you hurt her."

"Why must you be so fucking dramatic? We both know you don't have the balls to pull that trigger."

"That's where you're wrong."

He didn't bat an eye as he pressed his finger against the trigger, sending a bullet through Navarro's head. It was like time stood still as we all watched his lifeless body slowly fall to the ground. It seemed inconceivable that such a powerful man could be taken down with a single bullet, but there he lay. He'd only been lying there a moment, when a second and then a third gunshot exploded through the room. Navarro's men had shot Marcus, and once they felt certain he was dead, they turned their attention towards us. That turned out to be a mistake. They'd barely gotten a chance to aim their weapons when we fired our own, sending bullets soaring in their direction. When the last man fell to the ground, Alex rushed over to Marcus, and her sobbing continued as she knelt down beside him.

As she lowered her head to his chest, she whispered, "Thank you, Marcus. Thank you for everything."

To all of our surprise, his hand reached for hers as he muttered, "I couldn't let him take you back. I just couldn't."

Alex quickly lifted her head as she cried, "Marcus! You're alive."

"Not for long, sweetheart."

"Don't say that! We can get someone to help you." She

looked over to me as she pleaded, "Shadow! You have to help him."

I knew by looking at him that Marcus was right. He didn't have much time. Blood was pooling in his mouth, and he could barely breath. I crouched down beside her as I checked the position of his wounds, and when I saw that he'd been shot directly in the stomach, I knew his end was near. "There's not much I can do."

"But, you have to try something!"

Marcus gave her hand a squeeze and he wheezed, "Listen to me … Alejandra … I want you … to live … a good life … I want you to be … happy. You do … that for me, okay?"

"Yes, Marcus. I'll do my best."

"Your … mom would be … proud of you." He coughed, and it took all his strength to take in one final breath. "You're a fighter … never stop fighting."

Tears started to stream down her face as she watched the life drain from his body. When she couldn't stand it a moment longer, she reached for me, wrapping her arms tightly around my neck. "He's gone."

"I know, baby."

I held her tightly against my chest for several minutes as she tried to collect herself. When the tears stopped falling and her breathing started to slow, I placed my mouth close to her ear as I whispered, "Let's get you back to the clubhouse."

She took a step back and asked, "What about Jason?"

"He's coming with us." I turned to T-Bone and said, "Hey, brother. Give me a hand."

Once T-Bone helped me get Jason and Alex into the SUV, he walked over to me and said, "That apartment is on the third fucking floor. Cleaning this shit up ain't gonna be easy."

"No doubt. I'll call Gus and have him send over some of the guys to give you a hand."

"Tell 'em to bring plenty of plastic, cause we're gonna need it."

When he started to walk back towards the front door, I reached for my phone and called Gus. I gave him a quick rundown of everything that had happened, and while he was surprised by how things played out, he was relieved to hear that Navarro would no longer be an issue. We were still talking when he stopped to tell several of the brothers to head over to the apartment so they could help with the cleanup. Before ending the call, he asked about Alex. Like me, he was concerned about how she was handling losing both Marcus and her father. Even though I knew how she felt about her father, it couldn't have been easy to witness his death. Losing Marcus would only compound the hurt, but in time, she would see that it was his love for her that gave him the strength to do what needed to be done.

Once I got Alex and Jason back to the clubhouse, we took Jason down to the med-room so Mack could take a look at his injuries. After he got him bandaged up, Alex helped me get him set up in one of the empty rooms. Mack had given him some pretty powerful pain relievers, and he was barely able to keep his eyes open as Alex tucked him into bed. "I'm so sorry about all of this, Jason. I never meant for you to get involved in all this."

"There's no way you could've known he'd come after me."

"No, but I should've told you about my father … I was wrong to keep that from you."

"Yeah. You should have, and honestly, I don't understand why you didn't."

"I guess I was just scared."

"But you could've talked to me about it. I would've understood. It hurts that you couldn't trust me enough to tell me the truth." He closed his eyes, and I thought he'd passed out until he said, "But, I'll find a way to forgive ya."

"I was hoping you would say that." She gave him a quick hug before saying, "Get some rest, and I'll be back later to check on you."

By the time she closed the door, he was already sound asleep. She followed me down the hall, and as soon as we stepped into my room, she wound her arms around my neck, clinging to me for several moments. When she finally looked up at me, I could see the exhaustion in her eyes and said, "Why don't you lay down and get some rest?"

"Will you lay down with me?"

"Of course."

She crawled into bed, and as soon as I settled in next to her, she curled up next to me and laid her head on my chest. We hadn't been lying there long when she whispered, "Thank you for coming for me today. I don't know what I would've done if you hadn't come."

"Don't you know … there's nothing in this world I wouldn't do for you, Alex." I looked down at her as I said, "I never dreamed I could love anyone like I love you. You have me heart and soul, and I'll die giving you everything I have to give."

She eased up on the bed and leaned towards me,

pressing her lips against mine. "I love you, too, Mason … so very, very much."

As she laid her head down on my chest, I told her, "You scared me today. I was afraid something would happen before I could get to you."

"I'm really sorry. I didn't think I had any other choice."

"Why don't you tell me what happened?"

She let out a deep breath before saying, "He saw me outside by the fence. That's how he knew that we were trying to trap him."

"Did he tell you that?"

"Yes. He mentioned it during the phone call." She let out a deep breath before saying, "I still don't know how my father found out about Jason."

"He was a smart man. There's no telling how he found out."

With the tip of her finger, she trailed lines across my chest as she told me all about Jason's phone call, and how her father threatened to kill him if she didn't come to his apartment alone. She didn't think she had a choice but to do what he'd asked, and her voice was strained as she described seeing Jason so badly beaten. She was even more surprised when she found out Marcus was there. Her voice grew soft as she told me how he wouldn't even look at her, making her think that he was there to help her father. It wasn't until he brought out his weapon that she realized he was there to protect her. With each word she spoke, her voice became more and more faint. Knowing she needed to rest, I whispered, "It's over, baby. Just try to get some sleep."

It was then that she whispered something that made my blood run cold. "I wish I could believe that."

"Your father is gone. There's nothing more he can do to you."

"It's not him that I'm worried about. It's his brother, Josue. He's even worse than my father."

Before she could explain any further, she closed her eyes and drifted off to sleep, leaving me wondering if there was more hell to come. I was tempted to wake her and ask what she'd meant, but decided to let her sleep. We both needed to put this night behind us, and I knew that as long as we had each other, we could face whatever came our way.

ALEX

The days after the attack were tough. I was struggling to come to terms with everything that had happened. Losing someone you care about is one thing, but watching them take their last breath is another thing altogether. It stays with you, lingers in your thoughts and haunts you in your dreams. Shadow knew what that was like. Remembering the pain he'd gone through when Michele died, he arranged for Marcus to have a proper burial. He thought it might help me find some sense of closure, but even after his funeral, I was still having a difficult time. Shadow assured me that things would get better. That I just needed more time, but I didn't agree. I needed something to take my mind off of things, so against Shadow's wishes, I reopened the bookstore. I knew he was worried that my father's brother, Josue, would come after me, especially after I'd explained his connection to my father's business, but I was done living in fear. I wanted to get back to work and visit with my customers so I could find a sense of normalcy in my life again.

I found solace in my old routines, and with each day that passed, I felt the tightness in my chest starting to fade and it wasn't long before I was back to my old self again. I was pleased to see that I wasn't the only one who found comfort in old routines. I'd only had the store reopened for a few days when Shadow came strolling through the door. Like so many times before, he walked over to the counter and made himself a cup of coffee and then scanned the different shelves looking for the perfect book. It was at this point his routine took a dramatic change. Instead of going to the back of the store to read, he'd find a spot close to me and we'd spend our morning together. Those moments quickly became the best part of my day.

I was happy, truly happy, and things in my life were finally settling down. Shadow had me talk to Gus about my Uncle Josue. After I told him everything I knew about him, he assured me that the brothers would keep an eye out for him. Knowing they would do everything in their power to keep him at bay, I let go of my worries, and eventually our lives got back to normal. After spending the night making love to Shadow, I woke up with my head on his chest and his arm wrapped around my waist. There was no better feeling than feeling his warm body next to mine. With great hesitation, I got up and took a long, hot shower. Once I was done, I got dressed and headed to the bookstore to get things ready to start the day. I'd just gotten things ready when Jason came charging in.

He could barely contain his excitement as he asked, "Did you hear?"

"Hear what?"

"The Sacred Knights are going to be at Newman's tonight!"

It was good to see that all of his bruises had finally disappeared, and all his lacerations had healed. They had been a constant reminder of his kidnapping, and while he'd assured me that he didn't blame me for any of it, I couldn't help but feel guilty about it. As he stood there with a thrilled look on his face, I hated to disappoint him, but I had no idea who he was talking about. Having no idea what to say, I replied, *"Okay?"*

"Aren't you pumped?"

"Umm… I hate to break it to ya, but I've never heard of the Sacred Knights."

His mouth dropped as he looked at me with utter disbelief. "Are you kidding me! How do you not know about them? They're huge!"

"I don't know what to tell ya. I've been busy."

"Well, that must be rectified. You've gotta come with me."

I grimaced as I told him, "I'm sorry, but I can't."

"What? Why not?"

"I've already made plans with Shadow." I could see the disappointment in his eyes as I continued, "We're going over to Blaze's house for a cookout with the guys. You should come grab a bite with us."

"Nah. You go ahead. I don't want to intrude."

"Don't be silly. You know Shadow wouldn't mind. I think you're kind of growing on him."

"Really?" he asked, sounding hopeful.

Over the past month, Jason had made a habit of stopping by the bookstore at times when he knew Shadow would be there and had even come by the clubhouse a few times. At first, I thought it was just his way of checking up on me, but I quickly realized there was a different reason for his visits. Even though he'd never admit it, I could tell that he was intrigued by Shadow and the club, and the more time he'd spent with him, he discovered that he was actually a good guy—a guy he actually liked. I know he was surprised by the fact, but I couldn't have been happier. I smiled at him as I answered, "Yes. Really. You should really think about coming by. Maybe we could hit the concert after?"

"Okay. I think I can do that."

"Great. The cookout starts at six. I'll text you with the address."

"Sounds good." As he started for the door, he said, "I'll see ya tonight!"

Once he was gone, I hurried to wrap things up, so I could close the store early. I wanted to have time to take a quick shower before we headed over to Blaze's place. As soon as the last customer left, I locked things up and headed upstairs to my apartment. Even though I spent every night with Shadow, I hadn't officially moved in with him, mainly because there simply wasn't enough room for all of my things in his room. We'd tried finding a place of our own, but nothing seemed to suit me. Shadow had dropped several hints, letting me know that he was growing impatient, but I wanted to hold out for the perfect place for us to start our lives together.

After I got dressed, I grabbed my purse and headed downstairs. I'd just locked the door, when Shadow pulled up on his motorcycle. As I walked over to him, I smiled and said, "Hey, there handsome. I wasn't expecting you to come here. Is everything okay?"

"Yeah. Everything's good." He offered me my helmet as he said, "I had something I wanted to show you before we headed over to Blaze's place."

"Umm … okay," I answered with curiosity. I took the helmet from his hand and climbed on behind him. As soon as I was settled, he revved his engine, and I placed my hands on his hips as we pulled out onto the road. Once we'd picked up speed, I leaned my back against the seat and let the wind whip around me, and I couldn't help but smile. I loved the feeling of being out in the open. Everything around me seemed more vivid, like I could just reach out and touch all the different colors. I could've ridden with him for hours, but the ride ended when Shadow suddenly pulled into a driveway in the center of midtown. I turned to see a beautiful, dark gray bungalow with a beautiful white porch that led up to the entry way. There was a swing on one side of the front door and two wicker rocking chairs on the other.

As he helped me off the bike, I was surprised to see two familiar bikes were parked ahead of us in the driveway. "Who's house is this?"

"You'll see."

He reached for my hand, and without saying a word, he led me inside. As soon as we walked through the front door, I left Shadow's side and started walking through all the different rooms. There were hardwood floors throughout with fresh paint on all the walls. There were three bedrooms and two baths, and it had brand new tile and stainless steel appliances in the kitchen. While the house was empty and didn't have any furniture, I could image how fabulous it would look completely furnished, and as I looked around at every last detail, I couldn't think of a single thing I would change. I absolutely loved it.

I was just about to ask Shadow why he'd brought me to see it when T-Bone and Gunner came strolling in through the back door. Gunner looked over to Shadow with a big, goofy smile and asked, "Well? Does she like it?"

Answering for him, I said, "I love it."

"Did you check out the master bathroom?"

"Umm … yeah. Why?"

"Did you check out the bidet?" Before I could answer, he said, "It's got cold and hot water options, and I gotta tell ya, the cold water has got some power behind it."

I couldn't help but giggle at his enthusiasm. "Is that right?"

"It's awesome. Hell, the whole house is awesome. You should definitely buy it."

I quickly turned to Shadow and asked, "What is he talking about?"

Before answering me, he turned to T-Bone and Gunner and said, "Give us a moment, guys."

As they started for the door, T-Bone answered, "You got it, brother."

Once they were gone, Shadow walked over to me, and as he placed his hands on my waist, he said, "Once I saw it, I thought you might like it, and if you do, I'm gonna buy it … but only if you like it."

"Are you kidding? I love it!" I wrapped my arms around him, hugging him tightly as I told him, "It's absolutely perfect. I can't believe you found it."

"Then, that settles it. Looks like we're buying ourselves a house."

Before we left, we took another quick look around, and Gunner made sure to show me the bidet as we strolled through the enormous master bathroom. I hated to leave, but it was time for us to head over to Blaze's. When we got outside, I stopped, and as I took one more look at our future home, I was overcome with joy. Once I'd gotten back on Shadow's bike, I wrapped my arms around him and gave him a squeeze. "I love you, Mason."

He turned around to face me, and just before he pressed his lips to mine, he whispered, "And I love you, Alejandra."

Our tender moment was derailed when Gunner shouted, "Come on, you two! We're gonna be late!"

With an irritated groan, Shadow started the engine, and with Gunner and T-Bone following close behind, he backed out of the driveway and headed over to Blaze's. By the time we got there, several of the guys had already gathered around the grill and were watching Moose as he prepared his special BBQ ribs. After we said our hellos, we headed inside to see what we could do to help. When we walked into the kitchen, Kenedee was taking the beans out of the stove, while Blaze was gathering the plates and utensils to take outside. I walked over to Kenedee and asked, "Hey. Is there anything I can do to help?"

"I think I've got everything, except the deserts. Would you mind grabbing them from the fridge?"

"Sure!"

Shadow helped me take the various pies out to the picnic tables, and in no time, Kenedee and Blaze had everything ready to go. The guys were practically frothing at the mouth as Moose placed the meat in the center of the table, and as soon as Gus had given the blessing, they all dove in, piling their plates with food. Shadow and I had just sat down to eat, when Jason pulled up, and to my surprise, he hadn't come alone. When he started towards us, there was a beautiful, young blonde by his side, and from the look on her face, she was quite taken with him. I couldn't help but smile as I watched them sit down next to us. "Hey. I'm glad you could make it. Who's your friend?"

"This is Alice. We met at Newman's a few weekends ago." He turned to her and said, "This is Alex and that's her guy, Shadow."

A light blush crossed her face as she looked over at us. "It's really nice to meet you both. I've heard a lot about ya."

"It's nice to meet you, too."

"It took some convincing to get her to agree to come, but once I told her about Moose's BBQ, there was no way she could turn me down." He reached across the table and as he started making them both a plate, he looked over to Blaze and Gunner and said, "Hey, guys. How's it going?"

With their mouths full of food, they both answered, "Good."

Just before Jason sat back down, T-Bone leaned towards him and whispered, "Got yourself a nice piece there, brother. I'm impressed."

Jason gave him a quick nod and smiled. "Thanks, man. Just remember she's taken."

"I'll do my best," he chuckled.

Once he'd finished making their plates, he came back over to the table and sat Alice's food down in front of her and smiled. "See. It looks awesome, doesn't it."

"Yes, it does."

"It tastes even better."

We all started to eat, and as we sat there talking, I quickly realized that Jason had found his perfect match. They both had similar tastes in music, and whenever he got out of hand, she quickly put him in his place. I liked that about her, and apparently, he did, too. He couldn't take his eyes off her. I'd never seen him so smitten, and it did my heart good to see him so happy.

We had just finished eating when Jason turned to Shadow and said, "I owe you an apology."

Shadow's eyebrows furrowed as he asked, "What for?"

"The night after you helped Alex to her car, I told her that she should steer clear of you. I'd heard some things about your club, and I was worried she might get hurt if she got involved with you. After getting to know you and your brothers, I see how wrong I was."

"Appreciate that, but it wasn't necessary."

"It was. You make her happy, and nobody deserves to be happy as much as she does."

"Couldn't agree more."

As Jason and Alice got up from the table, he turned to me and said, "Well, I hate to eat and run, but we have a concert to get to."

I walked over and gave him a quick hug. "I hope you have a great time."

"Are you sure you don't want to come?"

"No." I shook my head and smiled. "We'll catch the next one."

"Okay. Suit yourself."

After he said his goodbyes to the others, Jason took Alice's hand in his and led her back to his car. Once they were gone, Shadow and I helped get everything cleaned up and put away. The guys were all standing around the fire, and I was expecting Shadow to go over and join them. Instead, he came over to me and asked, "You ready to go?"

"You don't want to stay?"

"We could, but I'm not sure staying out late is a good idea. We're going to have a long day tomorrow."

I didn't realize we had plans, so I asked, "Why? What are we going to be doing?"

"Moving into our new house."

"What are you talking about? We haven't even bought the house yet."

"I made a call to the relator. Offered to pay extra if we could move in right away, and the buyers accepted."

"You're kidding me!"

"Nope. The house is ours. She's bringing the papers by first thing in the morning, and once we've signed, she'll hand over the keys."

"I don't know how you did it, but I'm glad you did!" I reached up and hugged him. "Oh, God. There's so much stuff at my apartment! It's going to take me forever to pack."

"We have plenty of time for all of that." He pressed his lips against mine, then said, "Right now, I just want to spend the night making love to my girl. You good with that?"

"Yeah, I'm good with that. I'm always good with that."

EPILOGUE

There's no better feeling than having her in my arms, listening to the sound of her breathing as she nestles her head beneath my chin. She was perfect in every way. Her rosy cheeks and big brown eyes melted my heart. There was only one other person who could get to me the way she did, and that was her mother. They both filled my heart with a love like I'd never known, and there was nothing in this world I wouldn't do for either of them. Over the past few months, I'd made a habit of rocking her too long. Alex fussed at me, telling me that I was spoiling her, but I just couldn't help myself. Emma was just eight months old and still so tiny. I wanted to cherish these moments with her while I still could. It wouldn't be long before she was crawling, then walking. I knew when that time came, she would want to explore the world, and moments like these would be no more.

I glanced over at the clock, and when I saw that it was after midnight, I knew I had to put her down. I eased out of the rocker, and after I laid her in the crib, I waited several minutes to make sure she didn't stir. Once I was certain she was sleeping soundly, I went across the hall to our bedroom. When I slipped into bed, Alex rolled over to face me. "Is she asleep?"

"Out like a light."

"Good."

As I ran my fingers through her hair, I asked, "Are you going to work tomorrow?"

"I haven't decided yet. I was thinking I would let Alice handle things for the day, but I really need to place an order before the end of the week. I should probably run over there in the morning."

After we were married, I tried to convince her to move the bookstore to a better location, but that building held too many good memories and she couldn't stand the thought of leaving them behind. I decided not to fight it. Now that she was tied to Fury, there was little chance anyone would have the nerve to fuck with her, and my brothers and I would make sure that they didn't. Knowing she would be safe while she was there, I told her, "I'll be around if you need me."

"Okay, but just so you know … I always need you."

She eased closer, and an all- consuming need rushed through me as soon as I felt her body next to mine. Even though it was late, I couldn't resist having her. I eased on top of her, carefully positioning my knees at her side as I hovered over her. A knowing smile crossed her face as I reached for the hem of her t-shirt. "Can I help you with something?"

"You sure can," I answered as I eased her shirt over her head.

"I thought you'd never ask," she teased, knowing we'd just had sex earlier that morning. I widened my gait, giving her room to remove her panties, and once she was completely undressed, she lied still beneath. She looked up at me, so trusting and full of desire, and I couldn't imagine wanting anything more. Without saying a word, I pulled off my boxers and positioned myself between her legs. She looked up at me with her eyes full of desire as I brushed my throbbing cock along her center, driving us both wild with need.

"Mason," she pleaded as she wrapped her legs around me, pulling me forward. A deep growl vibrated through my chest as I thrust deep inside her. She felt so damn good and I couldn't resist driving into her again and again. My pace became hard and demanding, but she tightened her legs around my waist and rocked against me, encouraging me to give her more. I growled as I ground my hips against her.

I buried my face in her neck as I growled, "Fuck. I'll never get enough of you."

I thrust deeply, again and again, each move more intense than the last. Her head fell back as my cock raked against her G spot, causing her to tense around me. I raked my teeth over her breast as I took her nipple in my mouth. Every nerve in her body seemed to explode with my touch, and while I was enjoying every single moment of watching her come undone, my resistance was faltering. Her breath quickened as she clamped down around my cock, making it damn near impossible not to come.

"Oh, God! Mason!"

A deep groan vibrated through my throat as I continued to drive deep inside her. I could feel her imminent release, so I thrust harder, deeper, forcing her over the edge. Her hands dropped to her side and she fisted the sheets in her hands. Her orgasm took hold and I tried to fight it, but it was futile. With her body spasming around me, she wrapped her arms around my neck, and I felt her breath against my chest as I drove deeper inside her once more, finally giving into my own release.

Overcome with exhaustion, I collapsed on the bed next to her. Once we'd had a chance to catch our breath, I reached for her, pulling her closer as I said, "I don't know how you do it. Just when I didn't think it was possible, you find a way to make me love you even more."

"That must mean I'm doing something right."

"You're doing everything right," I told her as I kissed her on the temple.

"Well, just so you know … I love you more every day, too. Falling for you was the best thing I ever did."

"I guess that means I'm doing something right."

"Absolutely … except for one thing … spoiling our daughter." With a sexy little smirk, she continued, "When she becomes a total nightmare, you're going to be the one who has to set her straight."

"If I can handle the brothers, I can handle her."

"I hope you're right." A soft smile crossed her face as she said, "Especially since she has a little brother or sister on the way."

"What?"

"Yep. It looks like you're going to be a daddy again. You okay with that?"

"Yeah, I'm definitely okay with that." I placed my hand on her belly as I said, "A little brother or sister. That's incredible."

"Yeah, it is. Our life just keeps getting better and better."

"Baby, we're just getting started."

THE END

More from Satan's Fury Memphis coming soon.
A short excerpt of Blaze: Satan's Fury: Memphis Book 1
follows the acknowledgements.

ACKNOWLEDGMENTS

Natalie Weston –Thank you for being the best PA on the planet. You never cease to amaze me with all the things you do. Love you to the moon chick!

Ena and Amanda from Enticing Journey Book Promotions- Thank you for being such an amazing promotional company. You guys rock!

Lisa Cullinan – Thank you for being such an amazing editor. You always do such an amazing job.

Jen Allen- Thank you so much reading Shadow early for me. Your help meant so much to me, and I had a blast getting to know you at Mobsters, Motorcycles, and Mayhem!! You rock, lady!

Tempting Illustrations – Gel- thank you for your amazing teasers. I love them all! If you're looking for some amazing teasers, be sure to check them out. http://www.temptingillustrations.com

Neringa Neringiukas – Thank you for helping to make Shadow the best he could be and for sharing all of my books and teasers. You are awesome! Love you bunches!

Rose Holub- You are such an incredible proofer. Thank you for being there to catch all my many mistakes.

Terra Oenning, Amy Jones, and Daverba Ortiz- Thank you for continuing to post my books and teasers. You guys are awesome. It truly means so much to me that you take the time out of your busy day to sharing my work.

Tanya Skaggs, Charolette Smith and Kaci Stewart- Thank you for reading Shadow early and giving me feedback. Thanks to you, he's even better. Your support means so very much to me.

Wilder's Women – I am always amazed at how much you do to help promote my books and show your support. Thank you for being a part of this journey with me. I read all of your reviews and see all of your posts, and they mean so much to me. Love you big!

A Special Thanks to Mom – I want to thank you for always being there and giving me your complete support. You are such an amazing person, and I am honored to call you my mom.

EXCERPT FROM BLAZE-SATAN'S FURY: MEMPHIS

PROLOGUE

Excerpt from Blaze- Satan's Fury: Memphis

MEMPHIS, Tennessee had never been your typical city. While the melody of jazz music played down on Beale Street, tourists visited Graceland, and society folks had a drink at the Peabody, deep within the city, there were infamous gangs and rival MCs fighting to take control. Countless conflicts often ended with death and destruction, but when it was all said and done, there was always one that stood above the rest—Satan's Fury MC. With blood, sweat, and tears, they'd claimed the territory. In doing so, the club had made quite a name for itself and was considered the most notorious MC in the Southeast. The mere rumble of their motorcycles roaring by would bring a sense of fear to anyone who heard it, for there wasn't a single soul who didn't know the bedlam they could cause when they came toe to toe with an adversary.

Over the years, these bloody confrontations had become legendary in the city where the King of Rock and Roll had once lived.

I'd been a member for almost ten years—patched in just after my twenty-first birthday. From day one, I learned that even though we'd won many battles, the war to keep our territory secure was far from over. Every day there was a certain amount of bullshit to deal with: a fight to be had or a trigger to be pulled. It was just our way of life. For us, the club wasn't just a group of guys who put on second-rate cuts, pretending to be some kind of hotshot on a crotch-rocket. We were family through and through, and there wasn't one of us who wouldn't take a bullet for a brother. We believed what we had was worth dying for, and when someone put our family in jeopardy, we didn't think twice about taking them down—just like the night when we'd discovered that one of our runners had been skimming from the top.

I'd been asleep for hours when Murphy, our sergeant-at-arms, called my burner. I quickly answered, "Yeah?"

"Need you to get over to the warehouse. Runt's on his way to pick up Johnny and bring him over there so Gus can have a word with him."

Gus was the kind of president who stayed on top of things, and when it came to his club, nothing got by him —*nothing*. "At this hour, I'm guessing he's not wanting to talk about tonight's Cubs game?"

"Fuck no. That asshole came up short on this week's payout."

"How short?"

"Just over three grand."

"You're fucking kidding me."

Three grand wasn't even a drop in the bucket where our drug distribution was concerned. In a week's time, we pulled in ten times that amount, but that wasn't the point. Under no circumstances did anyone ever steal from the club—*period.* As I pulled myself out of the bed, Murphy grumbled, "No joke, brother. Now, get your ass over to the warehouse. We'll meet you there."

"I'm on my way."

It was one of those hot, sultry summer nights in July, and even though it was well after midnight, the air was thick with humidity. The wind could do little to keep the sweat from beading across my forehead as I parked behind the warehouse. I headed over to Runt's SUV and watched as he hauled Johnny out of the back, dragging his feet across the gravel as he took him inside.

Runt motioned his head towards the truck as he ordered, "Get Terry out of the back."

Finding the other man cowering down on the floorboard with a pillowcase on his head, I reached in and grabbed him, following Runt inside. We dumped them both in the center of the warehouse as we gathered around, watching Runt remove Johnny's blindfold. When Johnny finally got a good look at the man who'd kidnapped him, his eyes grew wide with terror. Hell, I couldn't blame him for being scared shitless. One look at Runt, and any man would be shaking in his fucking boots. He was our club's enforcer, and at six foot seven and three hundred and forty pounds of muscle, he was the biggest, most intimidating brother in the club. He had a knack for turning a man, big or small, into a pathetic, groveling mass of flesh, and this poor bastard didn't stand a chance —nor did his sidekick, Terry, who was sitting beside him.

When I yanked the pillowcase off of his head, Terry lost it. "Please, man. I didn't have nothing to do with this shit!"

"Um-hmm," I scoffed. We all knew he didn't have anything to do with his buddy's mishandling of funds, but we brought him along for the show, knowing he'd spread the word about everything that was about to take place. *I* wasn't about to let him know that, so with a condescending tone, I told him, "Whatever you say, Terry."

"I mean it, man. I got no idea what he did, but I give you my word. I'm clean, man. I wasn't no part of his bullshit." He looked over to Johnny and shouted, "Tell 'em, J. Tell 'em I didn't have nothing to do with this shit."

He didn't say a word. He couldn't. He knew he'd fucked up, and there were consequences to be had—deadly consequences. The second Johnny saw Gus walking in his direction, he nearly lost his shit. The blood drained from his face, and the vein in his neck started pulsing out of control. He knew what was coming. He was well aware that our president had a reputation for dishing out some pretty grim retributions, especially for those who tried to double-cross the club like he had done, so it came as no surprise when the motherfucker started to completely freak out. Like a wild animal, he used every ounce of strength he had to try and break free from Runt's grasp, but it was no use. He was no match for our enforcer, and he ended up with his face planted on the hard, concrete floor. As Gus approached him, Johnny started to beg, "I'm sorry, man. I'll get your money back. I promise. Just let me make a phone call and I promise I'll get it back."

Gus crossed his arms, causing his muscles to bulge as

they rippled down from his shoulder to his forearm. His fierce appearance was intimidating, to say the least, as he looked at him with disgust. "It's a little late for all that, don't ya think, Johnny boy?"

"I was gonna pay you back, Gus. I swear it. My girl just had a baby, and with all the doctor bills, I got behind." There was something in his voice that made me believe him when he said, "I wouldn't have taken it, but the baby needed some food, man … She'd been crying all goddamned night, and it was fucking with my head. The money was sitting right there … I know it was stupid. I know that, and I'm sorry. Just give me a chance, and I'll get your money back."

"So, you're telling me you stole for your kid?"

"Yeah. I didn't have a choice, man."

With a shake of his head, Gus looked to Runt and said, "Pull him up."

Runt gave Johnny a quick tug, and once he was up on his knees, Gus reached for his arm and pushed up his shirt sleeve, revealing countless track marks. Gus growled, "You're a real piece of shit, asshole. Blaming your kid when you've been using my money to buy fucking drugs."

Suddenly, panic crossed his face. "Those are from a long time ago. I haven't used in months."

Murphy shook his head and grumbled, "Only one thing worse than a thief, and that's a fucking liar."

Hoping that he could persuade Gus to give him a break, Johnny immediately started pleading, "Come on, Gus. I've been working for you for a long time, man. I've helped make you a lot of money, and I just fucked up this one time. You gotta give me another chance."

Gus sighed as he looked over to Johnny and said, "My old man was a farmer. He had over five hundred acres of land and the best stock of horses any man could own. We had us a couple of field hands, and one of them was a good man … had himself a daughter about my age, and he worked real hard to make a decent life for his wife and kid. But back then, life was tough and he fell on hard times. One night my father found him stealing feed out of one of our barns. Now, at the time, I didn't think much of it. I mean … what's the big deal about borrowing a little feed, but then, I was just a kid. What the hell did I know?" He reached in his pocket and took out his pack of cigarettes. As he lit one up, he continued, "My father was one of the richest men around with pockets filled with cash. Losing a little straw and grain wasn't gonna hurt nothing, so let me ask ya … What do you think he should've done about this guy taking feed from his barn?"

Johnny's voice trembled as he answered, "I think he should've given him another chance."

"I can see where you might think that, but like my father explained it to me—it wasn't the first time he'd stolen from my old man. It was just the first time he'd actually been caught."

"Not me, man! This was the first time … the only time —I swear it!"

"You and I both know that's not true." Gus pulled his gun from its holster and aimed it at his head. "A few dollars here. A few dollars there. That shit adds up, Johnny, but I'll set your mind at ease. I'll see to it that your stripper girlfriend and daughter are taken care of."

And with that, Gus pulled the trigger. When the bullet pierced through his head, blood spewing in all directions,

Terry dropped to his knees in horror. He brought his hands up to his head and squalled, "Oh, *shit*. Oh, *fuck*. You fucking killed him."

When he noticed Gus walking towards him, his mouth clamped shut and the room filled with a deafening silence. Gus slowly knelt down beside him and placed his hand on his shoulder. With a stern voice, he told him, "You don't fuck with the Fury, kid. You'd do good to remember that."

He nodded. "Yes, sir. I got it."

"Good." As he stood up, Gus looked over to Runt and ordered, "Get his ass out of here."

Runt nodded, and as he loaded him up in the SUV, Murphy turned to me and asked, "You good with cleaning this shit up?"

"Yeah. I'll take care of it."

Gus patted me on the back and said, "Go home, brother. I'll get a couple of prospects over here to take care of this."

"You sure? I can—"

He shook his head. "Go home, Blaze. We've got the run tomorrow. I'll need you at your best."

"Understood." I lifted my chin, and then started walking out of the warehouse to head towards my bike. My neighbor was sitting with my son, Kevin, and I was eager to get back to make sure he was okay. "I'll see you at the club first thing in the morning."

Before I exited, Gus yelled, "Be sure to tell Kevin I'm expecting to see that class project he's been working on."

"You got it."

Life as a member of Satan's Fury wasn't always butterflies and fucking rainbows, but there'd never been a time when I'd regretted becoming a member. My brothers were always there when I needed them. After my ol' lady died in a car crash, they stood right by my side, helping me carry the weight of my grief. I was just getting back on my feet when I found out our son, Kevin, was diagnosed with leukemia, and if it hadn't been for the club, there was no doubt that I would have given up hope. As always, they never let me down, and their support helped us both get through one of the toughest times in my life. I owed them so much, and through them I learned that having family isn't just important—it's fucking everything.

BLAZE

It was my favorite time of day: long before anyone else was awake and the sun was just starting to filter through the blinds. I was laying in my bed listening to nothing but the sounds of my own breathing. Kevin was still sleeping soundly in his room, so I had just a few brief moments to myself where I could begin to prepare myself for the day ahead; one that not only included getting Kevin up and ready for school, but also another big run with the guys. I just wanted to lay there and enjoy the silence for a little while longer, but my alarm went off for the second time, letting me know that my moment of peace was over. I pulled the covers back and got out of bed, rubbing the sleep out of my eyes as I headed to the bathroom for a shower. Once I was done, I got dressed and went into the kitchen to make Kevin some breakfast. Just as I was about to pour myself a cup of coffee, there was a light tap at my back door. Seconds later, I heard the rattle of keys as they unlocked the door, and my mother stepped inside.

"Morning."

"Sorry, I'm late. Your father had one of his spells last night, and I wanted to make sure he was okay before I left."

"Why didn't you call me?" I asked as I offered her a cup of coffee.

"I didn't see the point in bothering you. Besides, after he had a breathing treatment, he was fine."

My father had COPD, a lung disease that obstructed airflow to, well … the lungs, and he was on a shitload of medication that was supposed to help him breathe. Unfortunately, he refused to give up smoking, so he was only getting worse. "He wouldn't have to do so many breathing treatments if he'd just stop smoking."

"I'm well aware of that, Sawyer," she grumbled, "but your father has a mind of his own."

She was right. He'd always been one to do things his way and wouldn't listen to anyone, especially my mother. It was one of the reasons I was glad they lived close by. After I fixed my coffee, I turned back to her and said, "I don't know why he has to be so damned stubborn."

"You're one to talk," she said in a huff. "Leaving home at all hours of the night, doing who knows what and leaving Kevin with strangers. It's just not right."

"Angie isn't a stranger. She's been living next door to us for six years, Mom. She's a teller at the bank, and she goes to your church. I think it's safe to say that she can be trusted to stay with Kevin for a couple of hours."

"Yes, well … That doesn't make it right," she chided.

"Are you done? Cause I need to wake Kevin up."

"He's still asleep? We need to leave in twenty minutes!"

"Yeah, but I'll get him up and going," I yelled to her as I

started down the hall. I opened his door and walked over to the bed. "Hey, buddy. You need to get up."

His shaggy blond hair fell over his eyes as he rolled over and groaned, "*Ah, man.* Do I have to?"

I sat down on the edge of the bed and ran my hand roughly over his back. "Yep. You know how your grandmother gets upset when you're late."

"She's taking me to school again?" he whined.

"I told you last night that I had a run today."

He sat up in the bed and his blue eyes grew intense. "When will you be back?"

"Sometime late tonight."

"So, you'll be back in time for my game tomorrow?" he asked sounding hopeful.

"Absolutely. I wouldn't miss it, bud. You know that."

"Good, because coach said he was gonna put me in as quarterback," my little man's voice boasted with pride.

Kevin had wanted to play ball since he was old enough to walk, but that got put on hold when we found out he had leukemia. After losing his mother at such an early age, it was a hard pill to swallow, but he got through it—we both did. Since he'd been in remission, Kevin was bound and determined to make up for lost time, and when he asked to play peewee football, there was no way I could tell him no. I smiled as I stood up and said, "Of course, you are. You've got the best arm on the team. Now, move it, kid, or you're gonna be late for school. I'll have your breakfast ready in two minutes."

"Okay." Just as I was about to walk out of the room, Kevin called, "Hey, Dad?"

"Yeah?"

"Be careful today."

"Always."

Once I'd given Kevin his breakfast, I made my way over to the clubhouse to meet up with the guys. Thankfully, it didn't take me long to get there. It was just a few miles from the house, on the south side of the city. When I pulled up, the guys were done loading up and were standing around their old pickup trucks, and like me, none of them were wearing their cuts. Since we had joined up with our other club chapters and created a new pipeline, we would be carrying a load that contained shipments from five of our fellow chapters. We didn't want to draw any unwanted attention as we transported our load to Louisiana, so we had to get creative. Thinking no one would suspect a few farmers, Gus rigged up a couple of his dad's old horse trailers with hidden compartments under the floor, making it possible for us to hide all the artillery beneath the horses. While it took a little extra work, these runs had been a profitable venture between our clubs, and there were worse things in the world than hauling horses down south.

As soon as I parked my bike, I noticed Riggs, one of my younger brothers in the club, standing beside the trailer in a pair of faded jeans and a plain-white t-shirt. The ladies often called him tall, dark and handsome, but I didn't see it. To me, Riggs was just a smooth-talking pain in the ass. We'd both grown a habit of giving each other a hard time, so I wasn't surprised when I noticed the shit-eating grin on his face. "Well, good morning, sunshine. I'm glad to see you finally made it."

"Fuck off, Riggs. I'm twenty minutes early." Technically, I really was early, but some of the guys had it in their heads that everyone should arrive thirty minutes before the declared time. They thought it made them seem more eager or invested in the club. I thought it was a bunch of bullshit. If you want me somewhere at seven-thirty, then just say *seven-thirty*. It's not that fucking difficult. I got off my bike and started towards the others. "Unlike you, I've got responsibilities."

"Hey, *I've got responsibilities*!" he replied sounding defensive.

"Taking your flavor of the week home doesn't count."

"That hurts, man."

"Um-hmm," I grumbled. "Where's Gauge? I figured by now he'd be sitting on go."

"He went to track down Murph. It shouldn't be much longer."

I ran my hand over my beard and sighed, wishing I'd taken the time to have one more cup of coffee before I left the house. I knew the guys were starting to get anxious when I heard Runt growl, "Fuck, if I know, but he needs to hurry his ass up. I'm ready to get on the road."

Just as the words came out of his mouth, the back door flew open, and Gus came barreling out the door with Gauge and Murphy following behind him. He headed over to the trailers to give them the once-over, making sure they were loaded to his liking. When he got to the second trailer, he shouted, "Runt!"

An uneasy look crossed his face as Runt walked over to Gus. "Yeah?"

"Secure that second latch," he ordered before turning his attention to us. "Just got off the phone with Cotton. I told him we were right on schedule. Let's keep it that way."

Cotton was the president of the Fury chapter up in

Washington. He and his brothers were responsible for getting the pipeline underway, and there was no way in hell we could let them down. Knowing how important it was, we answered, "Understood."

Runt eased into the trailer, and once he'd locked the hidden latch, Gus gave his nod of approval. "Looks good. You guys are ready to roll."

"You heard what the man said." Murphy motioned his hand forward, "Let's move it!"

In a matter of seconds, we were on the road and driving towards Louisiana. Thankfully, we got down to Baton Rouge without any complications. When we pulled up to the old, dilapidated warehouse, Riggs jabbed me in the side with his elbow and said, "We're here."

"I see that, smart one." I scowled. "Now, move your ass."

As soon as we got out of the truck, Murphy went over to talk to Ronin, our distributor. We'd done well when we'd chosen Murph as our sergeant-at-arms. Not only was he a fucking badass who could handle any adversary, he was levelheaded and knew how to work the business side of the club. Murphy was respected by some of the most notorious criminals in the South. Once he and Ronin finished discussing the plan for distribution, Ronin's guys came over to help us unload. Riggs held the trailer door open while I led the two mares over to the side of the warehouse. With the horses out of the way, Murphy released the hidden compartment, and we started to unload. Ronin motioned us over to the backside of the barge and shouted, "Over here, guys."

He opened the hatch at the bottom of the grain container, and we stashed our crates in the space hidden beneath it, which would be completely concealed once it was filled. At this point, we'd all broken out in a sweat. As we headed back to the truck, Riggs wiped his brow as he complained, "It's hotter'n blue blazes out here."

"It's this fucking humidity," Lowball grumbled. He'd patched in a few months back, and over the past year, he'd proven himself to be a real asset to the club. Yeah, Lowball looked like the rest of our motley crew, every bit rough around the edges, but he was actually really fucking smart and had helped me a lot at the garage. He ran his fingers through his dark hair and said, "Makes me thirsty for a cold beer."

"You ain't lying. I could use a twelve-pack right about now," Riggs agreed.

As I started towards the side of the warehouse, I turned to him and called out, "Quit your bitchin', and help me get these horses back on the trailer so we can get the hell out of here."

Before we headed out, Murph went over to Ronin and shook his hand, "You know the routine. Keep Gus posted on the load."

From the dock, the barge would carry everything down the Mississippi River, and once it reached the final port down by the Gulf, it was up to Ronin to see that everything was delivered to our buyers. The club had been working with him for as long as I'd been a member, and time after time, he'd proven himself loyal to the brothers. Ronin nodded and said, "You know I will."

"Thanks, brother."

We'd been lucky today. We hadn't run into any cops or had to deal with any assholes who thought they had what it took to steal our load. Those made for long, drawn-out days that often ended with several guys having bullets in their heads. I'd say it was a pretty good day. After Murphy jumped in his truck, he put in a call to Gus, letting him know that we'd secured the load. Once he was done, we followed him back out on the road and started towards home, only stopping once to fuel up and to get a bite to eat. By the time we finally pulled through the gate at the clubhouse, it was well after dark, and we were all exhausted. After being cooped up in a cage for over twelve hours, we were all ready to stretch our legs and grab a beer.

As soon as we stepped into the clubhouse, I could feel myself start to relax. Something about that building just did it for me. I'd always liked the fact that it was once an old train depot that the club had bought and renovated. It took some work, but they created over thirty rooms, which included a full kitchen, a bar, and our conference room. It was pretty quiet when we got to the bar. Most of the guys had already gone home for the night or were off in their rooms having a run with one of the hang-arounds, which suited me fine. All I wanted was to suck down a cold one and get home to a hot shower and my bed. Riggs and I had just sat down when Murphy came over to us. He grabbed a beer and blew out a breath, "Damn. It's been a long one."

He'd just gotten the words out of his mouth when, Sadie, one of the hang-arounds, slipped up behind him. "Hey there, handsome. Did you have a good trip?"

"Um-hmm," he mumbled, obviously uninterested in pursuing anything with her.

She didn't take the hint and plopped herself down on

the stool across from him. "It's been pretty slow here tonight."

With his dark, shaggy hair and blue eyes, he had that James Dean look going for him, and the girls couldn't get enough of it. They all wanted to get their claws into him, but Murphy wasn't having it. He had his rules, and he wasn't breaking 'em—not for any chick. Ignoring Sadie altogether, he took a slug off his beer and turned to me. "You working at the garage tomorrow?"

"Yeah. Why?"

"I was thinking I'd bring the truck in for a tune up. It was riding a little rough today."

"Bring it on in. I'll take care of it."

"Thanks, brother." He stood up and took his beer off the counter. "I'll see you in the morning."

When she realized he was leaving, Sadie looked up at him with a pout. "You're leaving?"

"It's been a long day, doll."

Her lips curled into a seductive smile as she purred, "I could help you end it on a good note."

I could see the wheels turning in his head as he considered her offer, and seconds later he responded, "Let's see what you've got."

With that, she followed him down the hall. "That chick's never gonna learn," Riggs said while he shook his head.

"Nope." It was gonna take one hell of a woman to make him want more than a quick lay. After I finished off my beer, I stood up and said, "I better get to the house. If I know Kevin, he's up waiting for me."

"I'm sure he is." Riggs chuckled. "Tell him I said hello."

"Will do."

As I headed for the door, Riggs called out, “I’ll see you at the garage in the morning.”

The sun had gone down hours ago when I walked out to the parking lot and hopped on my Harley. As soon as I turned the key and the engine roared to life, the sound alone made the tension of the day start to subside. It was just me, my bike, and the road winding out before me in the night air as I pulled out onto the highway. Memphis was always a beautiful city, especially after dark when she was all lit up. I loved passing by the Arkansas Bridge and the Pyramid. As I pushed the throttle forward, it was as if I was the only man on earth; with the wind whipping around me, I couldn’t think of any better therapy. By the time I made it home, my mind was cleared, and I was ready to say goodnight to my son and call it a day.